ALEX
SLEEPY HOLLOW HUNTER
BOOK FOUR

SHERI QUEEN

CHAPTER 1
EXPECTANT FATHER

Aglow emanated from the bagel shop's window where Janda sat too visible for my comfort but enjoying the night and some much-needed down time before her due date. The light came from her, despite her efforts to contain it. Her skin had a luminescence like that of a golden moon in a clear night sky. I couldn't help but be in awe of her beauty.

Against my advice, her friends were giving her a baby shower. I'd been outvoted. To appease me, they waited until dusk settled over the town and the human residents had taken refuge inside their homes before starting the celebration. Her safety concerned me, but I couldn't deny her these moments. I shifted into my panther and slid into the shadows of the Sleepy Hollow buildings, ever vigilant about any threat to my wife and unborn child. A familiar scent drifted nearer, and I raised my chin and flared my nostrils, identifying it. I paused, waiting.

"If she sees you, there'll be hell to pay," Sebastian said, joining me in the dark corner adjacent to the shop. He wore a black tailored blazer but with the buttons undone for ease of maneuvering in battle. He also wore his hooded cape to help hide his overly pale skin. Neither of us wanted our presence known—not to the creatures of the night or to Janda.

I snorted and turned my attention back to the most important thing in my life. The old vampire had little to gripe about, since he was here doing the exact thing he admonished me for.

"I know what you're feeling, Alex, and I agree with you. Janda and the baby are our top priority. The paranormal activity has escalated, and I don't mind saying it makes me uneasy." He spoke in hushed tones and kept glancing at the small gathering of women inside the bagel shop.

The women laughed as Janda held up a tiny garment with a saying on it that I couldn't see. I smiled to see her so happy.

"She'll be a good mother," Sebastian said. He leaned against the side of the building and kept watch over Janda, Gwenn, and Angie.

It seemed Sebastian wasn't going away, which meant I'd have to shift back. My neck crackled, and my shoulder joints twisted. It wasn't uncomfortable. I was used to changing between my human and panther form. The process took a couple of minutes. I was in no hurry and didn't push the transition. I was capable of rapid shifts, but those took more energy, and tonight I wanted to conserve my resources.

"What does the Council say?" Back in my human form, I reached for the jogging outfit I'd stashed behind a crate and slipped it on.

"They're worried. We're not equipped to deal with

ghosts in general, let alone the parade of them funneling into Sleepy Hollow. It's going to get worse once October gets here. We have to contain this soon."

"I know." I caught myself clenching my jaw and forced my muscles to relax, then chuckled.

"What's so funny?" Sebastian's eyes narrowed, and his lips thinned into a tight line.

"This," I said, pointing to my biceps that flexed of their own accord. "I'm so damn tense that muscles randomly twitch." I rubbed my arms until the skin grew warm with the friction and the twitching eased.

"I would think Janda would find that amusing," he said, "or erotic."

I held back a bubble of laughter so Janda wouldn't hear me. "Sex is the last thing on her mind at the moment. She's so uncomfortable that even hugging is a challenge, especially in the sweltering August heat." I hesitated before expressing a concern I'd had for some weeks. "Can I ask you something?"

"Certainly."

"Is it wrong that I find her sexy even now?" I hastened to explain lest he think me a selfish prick. "I mean, I always think she's enticing, but there's something about her right now that has my cock standing at attention with the slightest contact with her."

With a sigh, Sebastian pulled over a crate and sat down.

I regretted confiding in him. "Why do I feel like you're about to give me a lecture?"

The vampire actually grinned. "Hardly. It's just that what you said brings back memories of Hulda."

"Sorry. I know you miss her." I couldn't imagine losing Janda the way he'd lost Hulda. The pain. The loneliness. As

I thought about it, I realized that I *could* imagine it and that was exactly why my life sucked right now.

He waited, somehow sensing I needed a moment to pull myself together. His tone became soft and wistful. "When you love someone as I have loved Hulda, there is not a single moment that one's cock doesn't respond to those emotions in times of proximity."

"That's not very helpful." I sat on a crate next to him.

"Probably not. It's the truth, though." He shrugged. "I suspect there are two things happening with you right now. First, your wife is about to have your baby, and that has somehow made her magic flare to the point that every ghostly entity within a hundred-mile radius is affected by it, so why wouldn't you be as well? All of Sleepy Hollow feels the energy. Some have no idea what it means or even recognize it. Others understand her magic is growing and are mesmerized by her. Second, you're in a state of heightened protectiveness. Your panther is ready to pounce on anything it deems a threat. Even your muscles can't relax. That cock of yours has its own muscles within it and is flexing them when you make contact with Janda. She's your mate. It's perfectly understandable."

I groaned, knowing he was right.

His look became serious, and he held my gaze. "Let this be a warning, Alex. You're constantly on the verge of attacking, so don't do anything rash. Don't let your emotions dictate your actions. There's a saying, 'Don't go off half-cocked.' Think things through before you act."

"Is that what the Council is worried about? They think I'll make things worse?"

He nodded. "Yes."

"How the hell can it get any worse?"

He put his hands on his knees and leaned toward me.

"The public has to be protected and kept from knowing what lurks outside their homes. Your actions can jeopardize all that we do to maintain that balance." He stood and took a few steps as if to leave then froze.

My panther caught what had alerted him, and I shifted in an instant. I snarled a deep, guttural warning.

CHAPTER 2

TRACKERS

The five guys who stormed toward the bagel shop didn't stand a chance. Sebastian swooped in and carried off two of them. They died instantly without uttering a sound. He hauled their limp bodies into the alley and tossed them aside. I noted all this while I had the other three pinned against the side of the building. It took every bit of restraint not to kill them. A quick sniff is all it took to realize they were human. Dumb bastards.

Sebastian returned, his fangs dripping with the blood of his victims. The men quaked before him, their bravado lost as their survival instincts took over.

"Wait. Don't kill us," one said. The others were frozen in place with their mouths open.

"Why not?" Sebastian said. An ominous growl followed his words that sent one poor sap sliding to the ground.

The only guy capable of talking showed his empty hands. "We don't have any weapons."

I moved one paw closer and bared my teeth. My panther wanted to rip them apart.

Easy does it. I thought the words to my panther form in

the hope our fighting instinct would relax so Sebastian could interrogate the attackers.

It wasn't *easy*, despite what I tried to convey. I forced myself to step back and take a guarded stance rather than an *I will eat you and love it* kind of posture.

"Okay! Okay!" the talkative one said. "What do you want to know? I'll tell you everything. Just don't kill us."

I glanced at Sebastian. His gaze slid to mine and back to the attackers. "Very well. Start with who sent you."

The men shrugged, looking to one another for an answer, before the spokesperson responded. "We don't know. We responded to an advertisement in an online forum and were given our task. The money would go into our accounts after the job was done. That's it."

"A forum?" Sebastian didn't seem convinced. "What forum? Who did you respond to?"

"It's a prank forum. Loads of people want to pull pranks on someone without being involved. I've done it a few times. You accept an assignment, get the details of the job and do it. Simple. Mostly, it's stuff like pretending to be undercover cops and raiding parties. Like tonight. It's a hoot to see the reactions you get, and it's easy money."

I shifted, standing naked in front of the men, who clamored to get even farther away. "It wasn't so easy tonight, was it? You stupid shits!"

Sebastian held out his arm in front of me. "Enough blood has been spilled tonight." He turned his attention to the men. "You were sent to scare the women inside? How did you know where to go?"

The man who had slid to the ground rose and appeared more willing to communicate now that his life had been spared. "Oh, simple. We follow the tracking device planted on the target."

"What?" I yelled, unable to contain my anger.

"Now you did it," Sebastian said.

The bagel shop door flew open, and all three women rushed out. Janda glanced at me and Sebastian and then narrowed her gaze at the men we'd trapped against the building. She turned that gaze on me and glared daggers. The gold in her eyes glinted against the backdrop of the interior light of the shop. She was lethal. She was stunning.

"I can't leave you alone for two minutes!" Her ire was in rare form tonight. "What the hell is going on here?"

Sebastian had the good sense to give her an apologetic look.

I was more direct, as usual. "These morons were sent to crash your party and scare you." I ran my hands over her clothes. "Someone put a tracker on you."

Janda pushed my hands away. "You're acting crazy. Really? A tracker?" She pointed to her shirt and spandex jeans. "Where would I hide a tracker? Seriously? I'm a flipping whale over here! There ain't no place left for this momma-to-be to hide a freaking thing!"

"She has a fair point," Sebastian said meekly.

I slammed the guy who'd told me about the tracker hard against the wall. "Don't lie to me!"

"I'm not," he said, gasping for breath.

The idea that someone had planted a tracker on Janda had my mind spinning all sorts of scenarios for how such a thing could happen. I concluded it couldn't happen. It was impossible for anyone to get past me to get close to her, except those in our inner circle. Even then, access had been restricted. I searched for an explanation but found none until I looked through the open door of the bagel shop and saw the presents.

"Those are a lot of gifts," I said. "Who are they all from?"

"How would I know?" Janda said. "I didn't get a chance to open them all before you went ballistic out here."

I ignored the men and strode past Janda to search inside. I pored over each gift, reading the tags and putting aside the ones from those we knew. That left about half a dozen gifts unmarked. I tore at the wrappings while everyone filed into the shop behind me.

Sebastian shoved the men into chairs at a nearby table where we could keep an eye on them. He tossed me his cape to wear. I tied the cape around my waist to cover the essential goods. It wasn't an impressive look. I'd been doing a lot of shifting lately, and my wardrobe was taking a hit. I had to come up with more spots to hide clothes.

"You think it's hidden in one of these?" Sebastian said.

I nodded, ripping open a second gift and starting to put them in a pile. There was a mound of onesies and footed sleepers, but no tracker. Then Hudson pranced over to sniff the remaining gifts. I let the cat poke at them without interrupting. Gwenn nodded when her cat pawed at one of the packages.

"He thinks something is off about that one," she said. She and Hudson did their telepathy communication thing. He meowed and sat next to the item.

I patted Hudson on the head. "Thanks. I've got it from here."

I took a breath and tore at the wrapping. It contained a single white receiving blanket within a dress shirt box. I ran my fingers along the interior and found a tiny lump in the box's corner where the flaps overlapped. Most people wouldn't have noticed anything unusual, but my job building safe rooms had given me plenty of experience. I knew instantly what I'd discovered. I carefully revealed a device no bigger than the tip of my finger and held it up.

"Holy shit!" Janda came over for a better look. "Who would have done this?"

"I don't know," Sebastian said, "but we'll find out." He turned to the men huddled together at the table where he'd made them sit. They paled at the threat in Sebastian's voice.

I held the tracker up to my nose. Whoever had touched it had been careful not to leave any scent. I was sure we wouldn't find any prints, either. I examined the box and the cotton blanket. No scent lingered. "They were good about not leaving any clues behind that we could trace back to them. I can't detect anything."

"Professionals?" Angie said. "Humans?"

I pulled out my cell phone and sent a text to Nick. "That's my guess. I'm calling in help to cart these dumb-asses away for questioning. Nick can handle them until the Council can interrogate them. I don't think they'll learn much from them. This was a well-planned attack. But why do it at all? What's there to gain by it?" I huffed my frustration and punched in a number on my cell. "I'll make a call to a tech guy that has done work for me. He'll be our best shot with the device."

Gwenn and Angie came to stand by Janda. "The whole town knew about the baby shower, despite keeping it a private event." Angie said. "There's no way to know for sure who sent the box."

Gwenn took the blanket and placed it on a table. "I can try a location spell. There's a slight chance the person who planted the device handled the blanket long enough for me to get a bead on their location before they dropped off the gift."

I nodded. "Do it."

CHAPTER 3

SCRYING

While we waited for Nick to arrive, Janda and Angie helped Gwenn prep for the location spell. Sebastian slipped out to move the bodies. I didn't ask how he planned to handle the situation. My guess was the dead guys would be found away from town and presumed killed by a bear. As far as I could tell, the other three attackers weren't aware their companions had died.

The police would eventually have to be brought in to take over with the online prankster-for-hire group. For now, we did things our way. I crossed my arms and stood behind where the men sat. The cape I wore diminished my authoritative posture by making it appear as if I had donned a skirt. Hudson sat at my feet and hurled hisses at the group. I knew there was a reason I liked that cat.

"Put the bowl of water over here where it's darker," Gwenn said. "It will give me a better reflective surface once we light some candles."

Angie placed one of George's bagel-mixing bowls on the table. Gwenn tossed herbs, as well as other things I didn't recognize, into the water while Janda lit the candles. Thank God George wasn't here to see how his baking equipment was being used. He'd wanted nothing to do with a baby shower and handed off his shop key to Gwenn to lock up when they were done.

The three women sat barefoot at the table and held hands to form a circle. After a few mumbled words pertaining to ancestors, they placed their hands in front of them on the wooden table. Gwenn pulled the baby blanket closer and stared into the water. Her eyelids fluttered a few times, then she bent closer to the bowl. If she saw something, it was news to me. All I saw was a bunch of stuff floating around on the surface.

I glanced out the window for what had to be the fifth time. My nerves were on edge. I wanted Sebastian to hurry and get his vampire ass back here. And where was Nick? I shifted my weight and rubbed my neck where a knot of tension formed at the base of my skull. I kept going back to the same question. Why send amateurs to disrupt a simple thing as a baby shower?

I couldn't figure out the benefit of a prank attack. Something didn't fit. I could feel it in my gut as I watched Gwenn's scrying attempt.

Hudson stood and arched his back, his tail fluffed out.

I followed the cat's gaze and gaped in disbelief. Several ghosts appeared just inside the front door. Their heads swiveled in slow motion, scanning the room.

"Fuck!" I moved between the ghosts and Janda—as if that would stop them.

Two of the captive men stumbled out of their chairs to get away from the apparitions. The third never moved. He just smiled.

The women abandoned the scrying. Janda shoved Angie

behind her while Gwenn made a figure-eight motion with her hands. She spoke words to a spell that seemed to catch the attention of the ghosts, who briefly paused. They weren't hostile. They seemed curious more than anything else.

Janda strode forward. "I can help you, but it has to be one at a time. Do you understand?"

They responded with sluggish nods. One took a few steps closer to Janda, reaching out a hand. She took it. I stared as the entity appeared to move through her. A cluster of light hovered behind her and then evaporated as the ghost disappeared.

The second ghost moved forward.

My eyes widened at what I'd witnessed. And she was about to do it again.

Hudson let out a yowl. I spun to see the prankster who had smiled barreling toward Janda.

God dammit. The motive for the prank was clear. It was the old Trojan horse trick, and I'd fallen for it.

Hudson launched himself into the air directly at the man at the same time I plowed into him. All three of us smashed into the counter in a ball of flesh and fur. Hudson latched onto the man's head with all four paws. His claws dug in deep. The man yelped but kept trying to get to Janda.

In my peripheral vision, I saw the two ghosts had formed their own protective barrier around Janda. At least they were on our side. I turned my full attention to the attacker, whose goal was now out of his reach. He tried to dislodge Hudson. I took the opportunity to land a punch to the attacker's gut that sent him to his knees.

Hudson hissed and relinquished his hold to jump to the safety of Gwenn's arms.

She stroked his golden-brown fur. "Good job."

Angie grabbed a chair and smacked it over the guy's head. He crumpled and was down for the count.

"Nice one," I told her.

Her eyes gleamed with the thrill of victory. "Thanks." She swiped her hand down the edges of her skirt and returned to where Janda and Gwenn stood staring at her.

"Remind me not to get on her bad side," Gwenn said.

Janda chuckled. "No kidding."

The two remaining pranksters were frozen in place with their mouths gaping in utter horror. If I had to guess, they wouldn't be pulling any pranks for a long, long time.

The spirits turned back to Janda. She smiled, put a hand on the first one's shoulder, and the ghost disappeared. She did the same for the second one, which glanced at her in appreciation and dissolved into the air.

I grabbed my wife and pulled her into a hug, or as close to a hug as we could manage. "I've said it before and I'll say it again. You'll be the death of me."

She laughed.

The door opened and Nick rushed in. His gaze took in the sight and he let out one of his low whistles. "Did you leave any fun for me?"

"No. But you can do clean-up duty." I gestured to the two frozen in a state of fear. One of them may have pissed himself. A wet spot had appeared at his crotch.

"Figures. Next time you go on the prowl, you can take me. I'm bored swatting ghosts away with those enchanted brooms Gwenn made for us, which, I might add, makes us look lame. Couldn't you have enchanted baseball bats? They're more manly."

"I'll keep that in mind with the next batch," Gwenn said.

The color normally lighting up her features was gone.

Her eyes had a haze to them, as if she was recovering from the trauma of the attack. Or maybe something had happened during her scrying. There was a crease of worry along her brow line.

"Fair enough," Nick said in a cheery tone. "If you let me know when you need the bats, I'll swing by the historical society with them." He eyed my cape-skirt. "New style?"

"I had to make do," I said. "In fact, I think it would be a good idea for all the shifters to plant more outfits around town."

"I'll pass it along. That will be even more important with the full moon approaching." He stepped over to the unconscious guy and lifted his head by grabbing a fistful of hair. "I've seen this fellow hanging around town the past week. Who is he?"

I glanced over at Janda. She looked spent after helping the ghosts and was unusually quiet while I was brainstorming with Nick. "No clue. Ask around and find out what you can about him. I'll see if Shawn can check the police database."

Now that the ghosts had departed, the air grew stuffy with the summer heat billowing in through the door Nick had left open. Janda stepped away and fanned herself with a menu she picked up off the counter. Her face paled, and she sat in a nearby chair.

"Are you okay, love?" I kneeled in front of her, and anxiety crept into my gut. "I think it's time for you to go home and rest. We're too vulnerable in town." I tried to get her to move, but she wouldn't budge.

"I'm fine. Really. Lending the ghosts a hand takes more out of me nowadays." She put the menu down and waddled toward the scrying station. "Did you sense anything, Gwenn?"

Gwenn shook her head. "Sorry. The scrying was inconclusive. Whoever is behind this knows how we operate. They left nothing to chance. I couldn't detect anything beyond malevolence. Someone is very, very angry."

I glanced at the two traumatized pranksters and the unconscious guy. "Someone human?"

"I got that impression," she said.

"That means we're dealing with more than apparitions. It sounds like the horseman could have found another weak-minded person to manipulate. We can defend against humans. The ghosts are a different matter."

Janda returned to the unopened gifts. "Nick can take these creeps away once Sebastian gets back. We should finish with the baby shower."

"That's not a good idea." I started to protest and was cut off by the stern look she gave me. I sighed. "Okay. I surrender. But let's not take too long."

She rolled her eyes at me and started on the pile of gifts from known individuals. Pink socks, pink blankets, pink pacifiers. The stash kept growing, and all of it was pink. My mouth hung open. I glanced from Janda to Gwenn to Angie. They all grinned.

"It was my idea of a gender reveal," Angie said. "What do you think?"

"No way. A girl?" My heart melted at the news.

CHAPTER 4

PROTECTIVE

The baby shower was almost over. My panther had nudged me a few times to move faster. There was only so much you could do to get a pregnant woman to hurry. The best I could manage was to assist with packing away the gifts so Janda could show them to me later.

The last item was a pink bonnet. She held it out in front of her. "Isn't this cute?"

I took it, running a finger over the hat that fit in the palm of my hand. I sucked in a breath as it hit me how small the baby would be if the hat fit my palm. "Assuming this baby doesn't get too cozy and refuses to emerge, our little girl will be here sometime in the next week. I can't wait to be a dad."

I could feel my protectiveness escalate and all I was doing was holding onto a scrap of pink fabric. What would I be like when I held my child?

"And then the real fun begins," Janda added.

I blinked away my worries about the future and focused

on now. That alone was enough to keep me busy until the baby arrived.

Sebastian came into the shop and stared at the plethora of pink. "What did I miss?"

Gwenn and Angie cleared away the snacks that had barely been touched thanks to the interruption of the pranksters. Janda took the bonnet from me and showed it to Sebastian. "It's a girl."

He stared at her. "A girl?"

She laughed and put a hand to her side. "Yep, and judging from how active she's been of late, I'd say we'll all be kept on our toes once she's born."

"If she's anything like her mother, then heaven help us. I hope you're ready for this." Sebastian beamed at me. "Whatever the child's temperament, the two of you have made me a very happy man. I just wish Hulda were here to be part of it."

Janda's joy deflated some. "Same."

Everyone focused their attention on the unconscious guy who was coming to. Sebastian bared his fangs as he calmly stepped over the prone body and lifted the man like he was picking up a distasteful rodent. Being human, the man had no tail, but that didn't stop Sebastian. He held the guy aloft by one foot, dangling him upside down. "It's time I removed the trash."

I stopped him before he could leave. "Before you drop him off to Shawn and Detective Brent, can you and the Council use some of your persuasive powers to dive into his mind and see what you come up with? The blanket didn't net us any leads, and the other two morons aren't likely to be very useful."

"Say no more. I'll let you know what we discover." Sebastian pinched the man near the back of his neck, and the guy stilled once more. "And who said I was surrendering him to the authorities?"

Even though I agreed with the vampire, I had to tread lightly with the locals. I let Sebastian's remark slide. "Nice trick. You'll have to teach that to me sometime. Is it a variation of a sleeper hold?"

"Yes. It is. Very astute," Sebastian said. He repositioned the limp body over his shoulder and left through the rear entrance that emptied into an alley.

I watched him go then took out my phone and messaged Shawn. "The police can have these two. Can you take care of that for me, Nick? I have to get Janda home." I was worried about how drained she appeared.

The perpetrators had slid to the floor, and I was fairly certain the wall they leaned against was all that held them upright.

"I got this," Nick said. "You should head home."

"Yeah, I'm ready." Janda glanced at her toes. "I swear my feet are starting to swell, but it's hard to see them over this baby bump."

Gwenn took a closer look. "You could do with an herbal foot soak. I'll put together an infusion packet and drop it off at the cabin after we finish here."

"Thanks." Janda gave both women hugs. "Never let it be said you ladies don't throw an exciting party."

"We aim to please," Angie said. "I think I'll stick around to chat with Shawn. We can use the prankster-for-hire angle to appease some of the townspeople."

She was a gifted public relations representative, but her attraction to the young cop played a huge part in why she loved her job.

I led Janda outside to the car Sebastian was letting her use. It was a silver Bentley, The Flying Spur edition. Speed met luxury in this sleek auto that I was thrilled to finally have the chance to drive. Sebastian's protectiveness over his collection of cars came close to how protective he was with Janda. Opportunities to actually drive one of his automobiles were rare.

Janda shook her head at me. "I don't think I can let you drive it. He said it was for me to use."

I gaped at her. "If you're serious right now, then I may have to break up with you."

She tossed me the keys and laughed. Then her eyes grew enormous. "Shit. I wet myself."

"Don't worry about it. You can change when we get home. The baby is super low and pushing on your bladder." I moved to help her into the car.

"I'm not sitting on those leather seats. Are you nuts?" Her voice rose an octave. "He'll kill me."

"Well, you can't walk home." I removed the cape from my waist. "Here. You can sit on this."

I didn't think it was possible for her eyes to get any bigger, but they did.

"Oh, no. Not happening. Your bare ass is *not* touching that seat." She wagged a finger at me. "Think again, buster."

I tugged the cape back around me and tied it with a quick snap of the fabric. "Then what do you suggest?"

Gwenn spared us a full-blown argument. "You do know that your voices are so loud they will wake the dead? And I mean that literally. What are you two arguing about?"

Janda pointed to her stretch jeans. "I laughed."

"Oh," Gwenn said. She didn't need any further explanation. "Hold on. I can fix that. I brought a change of clothes for you, just in case. Come back inside. You can dress in the bathroom."

"It's a normal bathroom, right?" Janda said. "'Cause, you know my track record for bathrooms at Mutther's."

Gwenn grinned. "Trust me—this is a standard rest room. No magic portal will suck you off to a different dimension." She frowned and glanced over at me. "You're not planning on any inter-dimensional trips again, are you? Because the timing would suck. Not to mention, I can't allow Janda to go wandering through portals at this stage of the pregnancy. It's bad enough you brought her through from the Underworld while she was newly pregnant." She shook her head. "Travel at this stage is out of the question."

I could feel my mouth hanging open. I held up a hand to halt her chastisement. "Please. The last thing I want to do is take my wife through any more portal adventures."

Gwenn gave me a curt nod. "Good. Then we'll be right back." She grabbed Janda by the elbow and steered her back into the shop.

A tour around the Bentley had my pulse quickening. I couldn't wait to slide onto the driver's seat, put my foot on the gas pedal, and listen to the hum of the engine.

Janda appeared in the shop doorway. The glow surrounding her was magnificent. Her aura held strands of gold woven through a tapestry of pale yellow. I opened my mouth to extoll her beauty when a flash of white appeared in my peripheral vision. Son-of-a-bitch. More ghosts.

"Holy, good God," Gwenn said.

"Nick!" I no longer worried about how my voice might wake the dead. The dead had arrived.

He raced outside to stand next to me. "Do we shift?"

I glanced back at my wife. "No."

He ran to his motorcycle and returned with a broom. "I've taken to hauling one of these around wherever I go." He exhaled a long breath. "I hate to say it, but one broom isn't going to cut it. There must be fifty of them. I haven't seen so many in one spot before."

"Neither have I." I didn't have time to get Janda into the Bentley, and the gathering of apparitions was marching ever closer. "We have to get her out of here."

Gwenn worked a spell, but it did little to impede the advance. She looked skyward where the moon silhouetted a fast-moving creature. It sped toward us, its wings flapping in powerful strokes through the air.

The dragon spewed flames across the front line of ghosts. They halted then surged forward once more.

"Mutther!" Gwenn shouted over the rush of wind created by his flight. "Save Janda!"

The dragon swooped low, cruising a few feet above the ground. In a deft motion of agility, he gathered both women into his grasp and flew off.

A collective moan erupted from the ghosts. A second later, they disappeared. The street was dark. The cold left behind by their departure sent a shiver down my body. I'd only ever felt this kind of chill in the Underworld.

I had a sinking feeling the answer to saving my wife and child would be found in the very place I'd recently escaped from—Prince Jasper's demon realm.

CHAPTER 5

BEACON

The Bentley powered through the curves and straight-aways with ease as I drove Sebastian's car to my home. I slowed only when I reached the narrow road leading to the cabin nestled in the woods outside Sleepy Hollow. My head ached with thoughts of my family and what I'd have to do to keep them safe. I was a mess.

Nick stayed behind long enough to fill Shawn in on the events of the night and the online prankster forum. He caught up to me now as we followed the road into the forest. The treetops wavered with the air current pressing against them, first one way and then the next. Mutther, in his formidable dragon form, circled above the cabin, making an invisible path in the sky and forcing the tree branches to bend as he passed by.

A glimpse in the rearview mirror showed Nick stopping to talk to one of the shifters in his pack. I took a deep breath to clear my head and get my shit together before I went inside to check on Janda.

Besides being tired, she was holding up as well as

expected. She was restless, but I couldn't tell how much was from the pregnancy and how much was from what she endured with the ghosts. Keeping her and the baby safe wasn't working well. We called in all the aid we could find, and Mutther kept watch from above. But we wouldn't be able to do this forever. While Janda made one of her frequent trips to the bathroom, I met Nick on the porch to hash out our options.

"Even you can't build a safe house to protect Janda from what's coming. Look around you. Our best shifters form a powerful barrier. They're all here for you, Alex, but it's not enough." Nick used his phone to check the cameras they'd placed along the perimeter of the property. Nothing was out of place and the line of defense was unbroken, but that didn't mean it was safe.

I pulled up the feed on my phone, double-checking what he'd seen. He glanced at me and placed his hand on my shoulder. The heat of his wolf pushing to shift sent a wave of guilt pulsing through me. They deserved better than to follow us into a battle against a foe who haunted our lives. Our intel was scarce, but there was no doubt that the Headless Horseman was taking advantage of the situation with Janda being a magnet for the spirit world. We were outnumbered, and the horseman wanted revenge. He was adept at manipulating humans who aligned with him for greed or power, including the stupid ones being recruited through the prankster site.

"I'll stand by you until the end. The others will as well," Nick said.

I nodded, realizing all too well that he was right. It made the sinking sensation in the pit of my stomach intensify. "I can't ask it of the others. Many have families. That's too much to expect from them."

A ring of shifters stood sentinel around the cabin. Damon's wolf pack joined forces with Nick's. They took turns guarding the small home that housed my wife and unborn child. Gratitude filled me with both hope and despair. Damon was Janda's uncle and a powerful alpha, yet he had sent some of his pack away under the guise of keeping their own region secure. I knew it for what it was—making sure not everyone died.

"How's it going?" Janda stood in the doorway, leaning against the wooden frame.

I moved in front of her, brushed the strands of white hair that fell over one side of her face, and planted a kiss on her forehead. "Everything is fine. Don't worry."

She quirked a brow. "You're a God-awful liar, but I love you anyway. This baby better get here soon. I can't reach my feet to put on my comfy socks. When I try, I pee. I can't even laugh anymore without wetting myself. Thank the stars Gwenn prepared for such circumstances."

Nick chuckled before I could warn him.

She narrowed her eyes at Nick and hissed. "Go ahead and laugh. I'd like to see you carrying a watermelon inside you that keeps pressing onto your bladder. No one mentions the damn uncomfortable parts during the last weeks of pregnancy. They want you to think it's all sunny days filled with glorious anticipation." She gave us both a steely-eyed stare. "They're wrong. Freaking wrong. Ain't no sunshine around here, folks."

I pursed my lips to keep from grinning. She didn't realize how beautiful she was, all lit up like a beacon. And that was the problem. Her witch energy had soared, turning her into a veritable lighthouse for the undead. They'd been coming at us for the past couple of months to reach her. Some we'd managed to deflect, but others had made it through. She'd dealt with them to the best of her ability, but she was still new to the magic.

"You should rest," I said.

"I can't. There's not a single position that's comfortable anymore. Besides, Gwenn left to get the herbs for my foot soak and some groceries. She should be back soon." She clutched her side. "Oh!"

My breath caught in my throat. "Are you okay?" I held her as she worked through one of the intermittent contractions that had begun a day earlier.

"Peachy," she said once the spasm passed. "I'm telling you right now. If that Headless Horseman comes my way, I'll rip him apart! I am in no mood for being messed with by anyone!" She turned and went back inside.

Nick's eyes grew wide. "She's scary!"

"Tell me about it."

Our home was nestled in a small clearing with acres of trees and underbrush on all sides. A narrow road was the only access point. We had shifters scattered throughout the area to keep tabs on the slightest change in the environment. After the first few spirit invaders got through our lines, we figured out that when one approached the temperature dropped to near freezing. We installed weather devices to track fluctuations that might alert us of impending attacks. The undead learned pretty fast how to knock them out, so now we had patrols guarding the weather equipment. That also meant our forces were stretched thin. We couldn't be everywhere.

I could tell Gwenn was near when Mutther veered from his loop around the house to greet her. His dragon dove below the tree line. I stopped checking the cameras to give them some privacy. They had little time together anymore.

A few minutes later, Gwenn pulled up in her car. Her

cat, Hudson, purred and scampered from the house to greet her. Nick went to help her bring in groceries while I remained at my station by the door.

"Wow," she said, coming up the steps, "You look tense. What did I miss?"

Nick lowered his voice. "Just the scariest hybrid shifter you'd ever want to meet, daring anything to come her way."

Gwenn chuckled. "Sounds about right for this stage of the pregnancy."

Nick put the bags he carried next to the door.

Gwenn stared at him. "You do know the kitchen is *inside* the house, right?"

Nick grunted. "This is as far as I go. You're a stronger person than me to tackle that momma-to-be."

She reached into a bag she held and pulled out a can of beer. "Take this. It sounds like you could use it."

He took it and popped open the tab then took a gulp. "Thanks."

She offered me a beer, but I refused. I swore off drinking the moment the first ghostly entity appeared on our doorstep. The truth was my nerves were more than a little frayed by the incident and now I couldn't relax.

"You sure you don't want one?" she said.

"Positive. I have to stay alert to protect my family. Being a dad is hard, and the baby isn't even here yet."

I listened for any sounds coming from inside, but all I heard was the gentle breathing of my sleeping wife. I relaxed a fraction, glad she could finally sleep. Her nights had become restless and not just because of the baby. She talked in her sleep while she dreamed of the Underworld. That scared the shit out of me. I worried the demon prince might somehow tap into her dreams. I now stayed awake when she slept and took catnaps during the day.

Nick drained his beer. "After seeing all Alex is going through, I think I'll pass on being a father."

"It's not for everyone," Gwenn said. "Still, a baby is a gift. And any offspring of Janda and Alex is bound to be special." Her eyes gleamed. "I can't wait. It's so exciting."

Her words sparked an idea and made my pulse quicken. "Do you think the baby will have Janda's ability to travel between realms?"

She paused, still holding a bag of groceries. "That's a good question. It's possible." Her brows furrowed and her mouth turned downward into a deep frown. "If that's the true, then it could be the reason Janda's magic is amplified right now."

I didn't like the sound of that theory. "What if the horseman knows that might be the case? What if he's after the baby?"

CHAPTER 6

TOUGH DECISIONS

There was nothing in this world that could prepare a guy for the feelings of inadequacy that emerged when he was about to become a father. Nothing. Decisions had to be made, and not everyone was a fan of those choices, especially the one who was carrying the baby. Much of the decision-making for us revolved around things we could plan for, like how to decorate the baby's room and setting up an education fund. While we had some differences of opinion, mainly about baby-proofing and decor, we resolved them without too much strife. I was confident in my role with such matters.

This was different. My confidence was at an all-time low. I was out of my depth. What expectant father wouldn't be if they had to deal with ghosts?

The impact of how we lived hit me hard. The world Janda and I were bringing our daughter into had special hurdles. We were shifters. We lived by a primal code of survival that our animal heritage had honed over the centuries. Not to mention, we both were Sleepy Hollow

Hunters, and that alone put added pressure on us as a couple.

I knew we needed to talk about the challenges we would face as a couple, but I was about to make a decision without Janda's approval. I figured it was an "ask for forgiveness later" situation.

Nick was still out front, keeping watch. He gave me a brief nod as I strode to one end of the porch to make a call. I kept away from the door and far away from my sleeping wife so she wouldn't hear me. I punched Sebastian's number into my phone and hoped the old vampire had remembered to charge his cell phone and would answer my call.

"Is the baby coming?" Sebastian's voice was strained. No one was left unaffected by the shitstorm going on around us, least of all him.

"No. Janda's fine. I wanted to talk to you. I think it's time to move her." I cut to the heart of the matter before he could get too worked up.

"What?" Nick said, eyeing me from the other end of the porch.

I motioned for him to be quiet so I could talk to Sebastian.

"Move her?" Sebastian said. "What does she need? A hospital?"

He rambled on despite my attempts to tell him what I meant. I sighed. I stared over my shoulder, wondering if anyone besides Nick could hear the old vampire having hysterics.

Sebastian's voice took on a fevered pitch. "You know that won't be a good idea and should be a last resort. I have medical staff waiting for my call should Janda require it.

Moving her to a hospital is out of the question. I can't imagine why you're thinking of such a thing."

"Sebastian." I raised my voice. "Sebastian! Stop! Just let me speak."

He paused. "Well, speak. What the hell do you mean by moving her?"

I raised a brow, even though he couldn't see my reaction to his swearing. He didn't cuss often, which just showed how rattled he was with the impending birth. "Calm down. Janda is not going to the hospital. I want her to move back in with you until the baby is born."

Silence.

"Sebastian?"

A bit of static and then a click. He'd hung up. I held my phone in front of me and stared at it in disbelief. "What the fuck?"

Mutther flapped his wings directly above the house. The next moment, he landed in the driveway. He shifted back to human and bolted up the steps. His nakedness made me realize I hadn't changed into my own clothes. I was still wearing the stupid cape around my waist like a skirt.

"What's going on? You were shouting," he said.

I shrugged. "Damned if I know. One second I was on the phone with Sebastian, and the next—nothing."

"I'm right here." Sebastian appeared on the porch.

"Jesus, man. What's wrong with you?" Mutther chided Sebastian.

"Him," he said, pointing to me.

"Why didn't you say you were coming?" I tried to keep my voice down, but it wasn't easy.

Mutther reached into a storage chest we kept on the porch and withdrew a couple of flannel shirts and two pairs of jogging pants. He tossed a set to me. "The skirt does you no favors, my man."

I untied the cape and handed it to Sebastian.

He held it at arm's length before tossing it on a porch rocker. "Keep it."

"Fine," I said, buttoning the shirt and pulling on the pants.

Gwenn peered at us from the front door. "What's going on out here? Any louder and you'll wake Janda." She stepped outside and shut the door behind her.

I huffed. "Well, now that everyone is here, I guess it won't matter if she wakes up."

"Now who's being melodramatic?" Sebastian said. "Get on with it and tell us what you're planning."

"It's more like not having a plan. I don't know how to keep Janda safe. I can't let the Headless Horseman take my wife and daughter."

Sebastian's fangs clicked into place, protruding like daggers. "That day will *never* come."

"Agreed," Mutther said. The slightest trail of smoke came from his mouth when he spoke. It seemed his dragon was of the same opinion and would fight anyone who tried to go after Janda and the baby.

Nick let out an ominous growl.

The tension in the air grew as our instinct to fight and protect rose.

Gwenn leaned against Mutther. "Does this have to do with our theory about the traveler ability being passed on to the baby?" Her contact with Mutther visibly soothed him so that his skin changed from his grayish-green dragon tone to his natural skin color.

Mutther wrapped his arm around Gwenn's shoulder,

tucking her securely at his side. "Crap. If that's true, then we have even more to be worried about."

I was happy they'd found comfort with each other. I had that with Janda. At least, until she discovered what I was about to do. "Yeah. I've been mulling it over, and it makes sense. Scary sense."

"I see," Sebastian said. There was an edge to his calm. A vampire, despite how calm they might appear, was not something you'd want to come across. With lethal swiftness, Sebastian would slay anything in his path.

Nick rubbed the back of his neck and started pacing. The floorboards creaked under his weight. He paused and glanced up at the rest of us. "This ain't good."

My brain finally began to work out a strategy. "Now you all know why Janda has to move in with Sebastian. Gwenn can strengthen Hulda's barrier to keep the baby safe. Nick can have scouts patrolling the woods for intruders while Mutther keeps track of the skies. Do we know anything more about the prankster site or the attacker who went after Janda?"

"I'm sorry, Alex," Sebastian said, "but the interrogation did little to shed light on who is organizing the human faction. It appears to be a coordinated attack where we can't connect the people involved to anyone higher in the food chain. I turned the man over to Detective Brent for him to file assault charges."

Nick bounced on the balls of his feet the way he did when he was eager for action. It was a quirk of his that happened when he had too much kinetic energy coiled up inside him. "I gave Shawn the tracker when he arrested the two pranksters so he could use it as evidence. He hadn't seen anything like it before. Between him and his detective uncle, that crew won't be going after anyone for a long time. Is there any news from your tech guru about the device?"

I double-checked my phone for any messages. "Nothing yet. I sent him pictures of the tracker. If I don't hear anything soon, I'll give him a shout."

"It's late," Gwenn said. "He's probably asleep, which is what we should be doing."

Sebastian lifted the collar of his suit jacket and peered into the surrounding woods. "You should all rest. I'll keep watch. When Janda gets up in the morning, we can pack what she'll need to stay with me."

I relaxed some, knowing Janda would be in good hands. "Thanks."

Sebastian patted me on the shoulder. "No thanks necessary. I love her, too. Now go inside to your wife and get some rest."

"Sure," I said. "Let's meet back here for breakfast, and we can solidify the arrangements."

Nick chuckled. "You can't fool us. You just want a buffer when your wife finds out what you did."

I shrugged. "Wouldn't you?"

"Hell, yeah." Nick went to his motorcycle and pushed it down the driveway before starting it up so it wouldn't disturb Janda.

Mutther got in the driver's seat of Gwenn's car, with Hudson and Gwenn riding shotgun. I waited until their taillights were out of sight before turning to Sebastian.

"What don't you want the others to know?" Sebastian said.

"That I intend to find a way back to the Underworld."

He straightened and came closer to me. I sensed the powered coming off him but held my ground.

"She won't forgive you if you go back there."

"I don't have a choice. The demon prince is the only one who has weapons that can destroy ghosts. I have to make a deal with him."

Sebastian shook his head. "That's not smart. No one comes out ahead with the devil's spawn. I don't like it."

"You won't have to worry about it if Gwenn can't help me connect with Maude."

Despite the darkness, the blaze in Sebastian's eyes was clearly visible. "You're playing with fire."

"Nothing new there." I turned and reached for the door handle. "Goodnight, Sebastian. Thanks for protecting my family."

He mumbled a disgruntled *humph* and went back to staring out into the darkness.

I crept into bed, careful not to disturb Janda. The blinds covering the skylight were retracted the way she liked it. I stared upward into the inky sky. Clouds drifted in front of the moon, obliterating its glow. In the distance, an owl hooted. The rest of the creatures kept quiet around the cabin. They sensed what was lurking beyond our sight and what I knew in my heart to be true—something evil was coming.

CHAPTER 7

BREAKFAST CLUB

"No! No! No!" Janda stomped into the kitchen and glared at our breakfast companions.

"Be reasonable," I said, following her to the stove. I bit my tongue. Not smart. Never tell your spouse to be reasonable. It never ended well. "Sorry. I take that back, but we want what's best for the baby."

I looked at the group gathered around the table for support. They shifted their gazes to their empty plates or their laps. No help from the breakfast club. I was on my own.

Janda pivoted to face me. "Do *not* tell me what is best for our child! I get it."

She yanked a frying pan from the cupboard, threw some butter into it, and began smashing multiple eggs against the metal rim. The gas flame ignited beneath the pan. The heat turned the perimeter of the eggs from translucent to white. That wasn't good enough. She grabbed a whisk and began beating the eggs until the yolks blended with the white. No sunny side up or over-easy eggs today.

Today we would be eating scrambled eggs. I counted

myself lucky she hadn't smacked me with the pan. That meant she was considering my proposal of her moving in with Sebastian. This was good. This was progress. I shut my mouth and started making a pot of coffee.

No one spoke other than to say thanks for the meal. They ate. They gave me sympathetic smiles. They left. I was alone with the love of my life and scared I'd screwed up big time.

"Fine," she said. "I'll do it." She put her plate in the sink. "And you can do the dishes." She strode off to our bedroom, where drawers banged and the closet doors smacked into the walls.

I breathed a sigh of relief and did the dishes.

The car was filled to capacity. She had crammed in all but the kitchen sink, or so it seemed. I marveled at how much stuff one baby required. I would have to consider building an addition to our cabin after seeing what she deemed essential items.

The drive to Sebastian's was quiet. I didn't know what to say. It was also difficult to see one another around the pack-and-play wedged between our seats. I helped Janda out of the car when we arrived. She put her arms around me and buried her face in my chest.

"I love you," she said. "I know this is for the best, but it doesn't mean I have to like it."

I brushed back the white strands of hair framing her face. "I know, love. I hate it, too."

She stared up at Sebastian's study window. "He doesn't even have real electric. One dumb generator. That's it. Seriously? Who lives like that?"

"Don't worry. He brought in more power options. Solar panels are on the other side of the house. He had an electrician working all night to upgrade a space to use as a birthing center and nursery. I can't attest to the cell coverage, but we'll make it work." I kissed the top of her head. "It's temporary."

She sighed. "Did he really go through all that to create a modern nursery?"

"Yup. He's taken his first big step into our century." I chuckled. "This could be a good thing for him. Besides, he's ecstatic that we're having a baby."

"Yeah. He would have been a good father. I wish Hulda could be here with us."

"Me, too."

It took several trips back and forth to unload everything and set it up in the nursery. Within a couple of hours, the space met Janda's approval. Her feet were swelling again. I set up the foot bath for her with the herbs Gwenn had provided.

"Better?" I rubbed the soles of her feet before stirring in the last ingredients.

"You're leaving," she said. She seemed resigned to being left alone.

"I'll swing over to the historical society to have Gwenn put together more of the herbs for you."

She leaned in for a kiss. "Thanks. I'll be fine. Maybe I'll take a little nap."

The room was serene in creams and pinks, but she seemed restless. I wanted to hold her and keep her safe. But my mind was made up. I had a battle to fight. It was one I had to win. If, in the process, I had to sacrifice myself to the Underworld forever and never see my family, then I could handle it as long as they were safe.

I gazed around the room. "It appears Sebastian spared no cost. You have to admit—he did a damn nice job."

She sank back in the plush chair and wiggled her toes.

"Yes. He did good." She waved a hand at me. "Now go, or I might find a reason to make you stay. And stop frowning at me. I'll be fine. If this baby girl wants out while you're gone, I'll cross my legs and wait for you."

I laughed. "Good luck with that one."

She was propped in the chair with her hands forming a heart over her belly. "We love you."

I blew her a kiss and took in every tiny detail of her. I'd hold that image for as long as I lived, maybe longer.

I met Sebastian on my way out. He walked me to the car.

"Are you sure there's no other way?" he said.

"Do you know of any?"

He shook his head. "No."

"Then this is how it must be. The first obstacle is getting through to Prince Jasper. If I can get Gwenn to use her witch magic to communicate with Maude, then I stand a chance of making this work." I hesitated. "If I don't make it back..."

"Not another word. You *will* return."

I let the matter drop. He knew what I was asking, and I knew his answer. That was good enough. I got in the car and rolled down the window. "Someone will keep you posted on how it goes. I can't say what will happen, but if I make contact with Maude, she may have to act quickly. The underground ferryman route may be my only shot at getting back into the Underworld. Even then, there's no telling how the demon prince will react. I'm counting on his debt to Janda, but you never know."

"Nothing is a given in life, Alex. Treasure each moment as if it's your last. That's all any of us can do. Godspeed and good luck."

I gave him a sideways glance. "I didn't figure you for a

God-fearing man, but I'll take the good luck. We can use all we can get."

I drove down his driveway and felt the barrier contract around me. It hadn't done that with Janda present. Sebastian had enhanced all security measures, both magical and technological. That reminded me of my contact concerning the tracking device. I dialed his number as I got onto the main road heading into Sleepy Hollow.

He picked up on the first ring. "Sid here. This is not a recording. Don't leave a message." He laughed at his joke.

"Funny," I said. "What do you have for me?"

His laughter trailed off, and he sighed. "It's not good, Alex."

"Never is. How bad is it?"

He must have put the phone down because I heard him shuffle some papers and grumble about needing a better filing system. Sid didn't own a filing cabinet. He didn't actually need one. The guy was a walking encyclopedia with a photographic memory.

"Sid? What's going on?"

The shuffling stopped. Sid picked up the phone. "Yeah. Sorry. I had to re-read this letter I found stuck under the downstairs door the gamers use."

"A letter?"

"That's what I said. An actual piece of paper. It was shoved under my door."

"Really? That's odd. What's it say?" My foot hit the brake, and I did a U-turn in the middle of the road. I was making a stop at Sid's. "Never mind. I'm coming to you. I want to see this for myself. Did you touch it?"

"That's a stupid thing to ask. How else was I going to pick it up?"

"Okay, fine, Sid. You know what I mean. Did you contaminate it?"

"That's an even more stupid question. Of course not. Christ, Alex. Get a grip. I used gloves." He paused. "You on your way?"

"Yep." I floored it, and the car lurched forward. "Give me ten."

CHAPTER 8

MAGICAL TECH

Sid, my tech guru, lived in an abandoned warehouse for years before he bought the entire building. He made a crap ton of money after he sold a microchip design to one of the big Silicon Valley companies. He bought the brick structure for cheap because half the pipes for the plumbing leaked and the other half didn't even exist. Sid didn't care. He fixed the bare minimum to make the place habitable and called it good enough.

He figured owning an entire building meant he didn't have to deal with neighbors. Yet he had a steady stream of gamer buds coming and going at all hours of the day and night. The gaming computers were all on the first floor. Sid monitored things using numerous strategically placed cameras. I met him when he asked me to build him a safe room on the top floor. Sid was different. He was human and an absolute genius. His appearance screamed nerd. He was a great friend.

I drove into the parking garage beneath the structure and entered a passcode that allowed me to open the security gate. I wound my way to the topmost level, parked, and strode to the elevator.

An intercom was stationed on the wall. I pushed the black button and spoke into the unit. "I'm here. Let me in."

A faint buzz echoed from the speaker set within the concrete wall. A static-filled voice spoke. "Enter if you dare." He tried to make his voice sound creepy. It didn't work.

"You're just full of laughs today, Sid. Come on. Open up." I waited for a moment and heard the click of a locking mechanism. The elevator door opened. There were three buttons on the inside—pretty standard. I didn't touch them. They were fake. You could push them all day and go nowhere. You'd think it was broken, but it wasn't. This was a fake elevator. I expected this. After all, I was the one who had built his secure space. Cameras swiveled on rotating arms to catch every angle inside the compartment. No one could enter without being seen. Just one more layer of security.

The panels opposite me slid apart, and I stepped inside Sid's apartment. He'd kept the open layout where all but his bathroom was contained in one large area. Specially tinted floor-to-ceiling windows filled two sides of the apartment. He had a fantastic view of the other industrial buildings in the area, yet no one could see inside his home. He had complete privacy. That was another one of my touches.

"Hey, Alex," he said. "What have you gotten yourself into now?"

"What do you mean? I haven't done anything—lately." I grinned and slapped him on the back. "Show me what you found."

"Well, it's kind of hard to find much when you haven't actually given me the device."

"I gave you a picture. That should count for something. Are you telling me you couldn't find anything?"

"I didn't say that," Sid said. "It wasn't easy, though. Here, take a look at this."

He handed me a pair of gloves. Once I put them on, he handed me the paper. I held it by the edges and read what it said. "It says 'magic'? What does that mean?"

Sid pointed to a small image sketched in one corner of the paper. "This is what it means. Does that image look familiar?" He grabbed another paper, a printout of the device I'd sent him.

"Holy shit. They're the same." I peered closer at the drawing and then at the photo of the actual tracking device.

"Well, duh," Sid said. "That's because they are the same. Someone is being very careful about what they're divulging to us. They assume we'd recognize the drawing and that the word 'magic' would mean something to us. Does it mean anything to you?"

I thought about what he said. Magic and technology. Combined. "Are you implying that the tracker device works through magic?"

Sid shrugged. "I'm thinking maybe so." He moved to a table with papers scattered about its surface. From beneath one pile, he withdrew an issue of a technological innovations magazine. It depicted a man in a dark suit holding a device like the one that had been planted inside the shower gift.

"Who's Stephan Turner?" I put the paper I'd been holding down and focused on the man's face in the magazine. "He seems familiar. Should I know him?"

"You know his father. The prince from the Underworld."

"Are you joking? How do you know that?"

Despite being in a secure room, Sid glanced around. He

lowered his voice. "I've had my eye on Turner for a long time. He's gifted and has connections. I've met him once or twice at tech expo after-parties. He's a big partier. Can't hold his drink. He babbles when he's intoxicated. Most people would attribute his claims of being the son of a demon prince as a drunk spouting off."

"But not you," I said.

"Not me." Sid sat on a metal barstool that he'd positioned in front of a drafting table. Blueprints of various inventions he was working on got shoved aside to make room for a large piece of blank paper. He began drawing a series of images similar to those of the tracker. But in his drawings, he added a small stone to the center of the device. "Brimstone holds power," he said.

The world seemed to spin for a few moments before righting itself. "Magical power."

Sid turned in his seat to face me. "Exactly."

I stared at the image of Stephan Turner and the tracking device. "But we know from the demon prince that only brimstone he infused with his own magic has power, so does his son hold the same magical ability?"

Sid shook his head. "I don't think so. If that was the case, then Stephan would be one of those most formidable men in the industry. He's smart, but not enough to be in the upper echelon of the tech world. My guess is he smuggled infused brimstone out of the Underworld or dearest Daddy gave it to him."

"Shit!" I wanted Jasper to give me weapons to fight the ghost invasion, and here was the demon's son living in the region around Sleepy Hollow. "How dangerous is Turner? Could he be the one attacking Janda through the prankster site?"

The laptop on the table whirred to life with the deft

keystrokes Sid tapped into it. "Let's see what our buddy Turner has been up to. He's arrogant. If he believes he's untouchable, then he's likely to be sloppy."

Various chat forum windows opened to reveal Stephan Turner's logo, a devil's face, staring back at us. Most of it was rubbish. Stupid bragging about his tech prowess. The guy probably thought his dick was big, too.

"There," I pointed to one of the chats. "He says, 'seek thy power with stones of fire and brimstone,' and it lists the prankster site. There's no link to it, just a mention to follow him. Geez, the guy's a whacko."

"That's him. A real Pandora's box of shit." Sid scrolled through more chat forums until he found the private link for the prankster site. "Bingo, dingo! Here we go!"

He double-downed on his security firewall and incognito status. It wouldn't do to tip our hand too soon. I leaned over his shoulder as he navigated the prankster site.

"I'm beginning to think your pal Turner runs this site. He has money to toss around and hire ignorant ass-hats to do his bidding." I patted Sid on the shoulder. "This is good stuff. But reaching dear old demon Daddy through Turner wouldn't be a good idea. I don't want a middle-man compromising an already tricky deal."

"If Stephan thought there was something to gain, he'd sacrifice his own mother, so best to go the more direct route." Sid kept scrolling through tons of content. "This is gonna take a while."

"What about his mother? Who is she?" I wondered what type of woman slept with a demon. I knew for a fact Jasper had been confined for a couple of hundred years. "How old is Turner?"

"It's hard to say. He lists his birthday as October 31, but no year. A half-demon might have a longer life-span than the average person. His mother had to be human. I'll dig into hospital databases to see if there's a record of his birth."

My mind drifted back to Janda. Time was running out for me to get to the Underworld and, hopefully, back before she gave birth.

"Okay," I said. "Keep digging. I'm going to the historical society to see Gwenn. She's the only one who might get me an audience with Jasper."

"Good luck," Sid said.

"Thanks." I passed through the hidden elevator door and hurried to my car, texting Gwenn to let her know I was on my way to see her. I took an alternate route to Sleepy Hollow to buy myself a little time to think. I wanted to process what I'd learned before tackling my plan to meet with Jasper. Yeah. I had to be crazy to make a deal with a demon prince.

CHAPTER 9

THROUGH THE VEIL

The day was evaporating faster than water in a sauna. I was feeling the heat—not in a pleasant way. Magic tech, half-demons, and a pregnant wife. Not to mention I had a crib to put together. Life kept me busy with all sorts of twists and turns. At least I knew more now than I had this morning. I just didn't know what to do with the knowledge I'd gained.

Note to self—*remember the herbs for the foot soak.* I put it on my mental to-do list as I swung into a parking spot behind Gwenn's car. I chuckled at her license plate— HUDSON. As many times as I'd seen that plate, it never got old.

Gwenn was in the front parlor, cleaning. Hudson pranced over to me when I entered and rubbed against my leg until I bent to scratch him behind his ears. Satisfied, he purred and trotted off down the hall.

"Hey," Gwenn said. She cleared off a chair at a small card table. "Have a seat. Can I get you a drink? Water, lemonade?"

"Water would be great. Thanks."

She went off toward the kitchen. I surveyed the room that she'd been diligently trying to get back into some sort of order to prepare for the historical society's reopening. "You've made good progress."

"Thanks," she poked her head around the corner, "but there's tons left to do. Cookies?" She showed me a plate of chocolate chip cookies.

"Nah. I'm good. Just the water."

She returned and settled into a chair across from me, enjoying a bite of her cookie. "I think better with chocolate," she said, grinning.

I grinned back. "So does Janda."

Her gaze held a patient, expectant quality. Yet, despite the silent encouragement, I remained at a loss, unsure of where to start.

"Would you like a tarot reading?" She picked up a deck of mystical cards and shuffled.

"Not today."

She put the deck off to the side. "Suit yourself. But I'm guessing you had a reason for coming without Janda."

"Yes. That would be correct. This is something I prefer Janda didn't have to worry about right now."

"That's okay. This is a no-judgment zone. How can I help?"

Hudson meowed in the next room. Gwenn quirked a brow. "Hudson seems to think you're a man on the edge of doing something you might regret later. Is that true?"

I laughed. "Later? I regret it already."

"Then you've made up your mind. What do you need me to do?"

My gaze never faltered because it was true. "I need you

to contact a spirit so I can find access back to the Underworld."

She straightened. "Oh, my."

"Yeah," I said. "That's why Janda can't know about it. I have to act fast, as in now."

Gwenn bit her lip. "I'll require time to prepare."

I leaned forward. "How much? I'm kind of running out of that commodity."

She gazed out the window at the fading light. "Thirty minutes. I suggest you call your wife and tell her something. She'll be worried about you if you don't get back tonight. This is serious stuff, Alex. There's no telling how this will go. It could go very, very badly."

"I'm aware and I'm ready. By the way, Janda asked for more bath herbs. If I'm not around to take them to her, will you?" I almost choked on the words. Life without my wife and daughter would not be living. I realized we hadn't even decided on a name for the baby.

Gwenn bustled to clear some space at the table and laid out a number of crystals. She also placed a bowl of water out as well. I heard her talking on her phone, but I wasn't sure what she was saying because I'd already dialed Janda, and my phone was ringing.

"I was wondering when you'd call," Janda said, answering on the first ring. She didn't sound cross, just tired. "Are you okay?"

"It's been a busy day," I said. "Wait until you hear what Sid told me. You are going to flip."

We spent the next ten or so minutes hashing over what he'd said. Both of us were convinced that Stephan Turner was working with the horseman. Neither of us had any experience with a half-demon, so I said I'd ask Mutther about it. She was going to discuss it with Sebastian.

"Okay, love. I have to go." My stomach was in knots.

"Oh, did you ask Gwenn about the herbs?"

"Yes, love. She's going to get another batch together. Is it helping the swelling?"

"Not overly, but it feels good. It also gives me something to do. I swear the waiting is the hardest part of this stage of the pregnancy." She chuckled. "I tried to rearrange the nursery, but Sebastian stopped me. He says I should rest while I can. I suppose he has a point."

"What if you start a list of baby names? Have you seen how many name sites there are? Sorting through those will take ages. You might want to start tonight." I was grasping at straws in the hope she would latch onto something that would keep her from focusing on my absence and the ghosts parading through Sleepy Hollow every night.

"Good idea. I'll start right after I talk to Sebastian. He's been harassing the poor shifters on duty to the point Uncle Damon stopped by to tell him to back off. So, Sebastian left to do Council business, and Uncle Damon is here. I'm getting ready to whoop his butt at poker." Her tone softened. "Don't take too long, Alex. I miss having you near me."

"Same, love. Same. I'll do my best to get back soon. I love you."

Ending the call was like cutting off a limb. If I didn't make it back from the Underworld, I'd be stuck in the realm of the dead and never be whole again.

As soon as I stepped over the threshold, I heard voices. I also smelled cinnamon and lemongrass. Gwenn had incense burning in several places around the room. The parlor draperies had been closed. The atmosphere was that of stepping inside a fortune teller's tent at the county fair. But Gwenn was not a fortune teller. She was a gifted witch.

"Come in," Gwenn said. "Join us at the table. I'm almost ready."

I glanced at the familiar faces of Mutther, Nick, and Sebastian. "Why are they here?"

"Gwenn called us to be sitters," Sebastian said. "Are you telling me you want to reach the spirit realm but know nothing of mediums and sitters?"

I sat in the only empty seat at the table. "I'm sure Gwenn has that all covered." She had created such an inviting space that I prayed Maude's spirit would come and join us. The table cloth was black; candles were arranged in the center—white ones, blue, violet, and several orange ones. All lit and flickering.

Sebastian saw me staring at the candles. "We decided one white candle was plenty. No need to call too many spirits with them gallivanting all over town. The blue candle enhances the communication, while the violet one increases the psychic power. And all those orange ones? They keep the bad spirits away."

"Let's hope they work," I said. "Maybe we should get a bunch of orange ones for the nursery." I added that to my list.

"That's an excellent idea," Gwenn said. She had pulled a shawl over her shoulders and sat on my left. "Make sure all your phones are off, and then we can begin by holding hands to strengthen the energy in our circle."

We did as she said. There were several crystals on the table in front of Gwenn. She released my hand to pick one up and place it on a holder in front of her.

After several minutes of utter silence, Gwenn spoke. "Oh, kind spirits send us only the blessed and bright. We claim protection for those gathered at our table and banish evil beings from here. Please, Maude, hear us and join our circle."

At first, nothing happened. Then the flames wavered. The white candle blew out when a quick wisp of air reached it. We held hands again, reforming the circle. Gwenn spoke in a low voice. It was not Maude who had come through the veil of the spirit world. It was Reggie.

CHAPTER 10

OUR GUIDE

All of us jumped but kept hold of one another's hand. The orange candles remained lit, as did the blue and violet.

"Is this normal?" Nick asked. He kept his voice to a whisper.

"All is well," Gwenn said. "Join us, Reggie. Tell us why Maude did not come."

The white crystal pendulum swung back and forth in front of her. A faint voice, like someone talking through a tunnel, filled the air. The crystal had become a transmitter—a tiny two-way radio tuning in to the spiritual plane. I wasn't expecting that at all. I assumed Gwenn would be the conduit but kept my thoughts to myself.

"I am who you need. I freely offer my services as payment for past wrongs. Do you accept?" Reggie's voice ebbed and flowed on the air currents.

"Yes," I said, before Gwenn could stop me. I didn't care who answered my call for help. Reggie was the new underground ferryman. If anyone could get me back to the Underworld, it was him.

Silence followed. The others shot me nasty looks for interrupting.

I wasn't about to let the connection go. "Reggie? It's Alex. Can you hear me?"

Static. Garbled words poured from the crystal. More static. I gazed at Gwenn, imploring her to do something. She quickly lit a second blue candle. The transmission strengthened enough for us to hear Reggie more clearly.

"I hear you, Alex."

I let out a breath. "Thank the Gods. Reggie, I need you to help me get back into the Underworld. Can you do that? Can we use the underground ferryman route?"

"Sorry, Alex. I want to assist. I do, but the route has been under siege by the demon prince."

Mutther sat on my other side. I almost released my grip on his hand, but he sensed me slipping and held me tighter. I nodded my thanks.

"What about Maude?" I said. "Does she have a new route?"

Reggie hummed a little pirate tune. I glanced around at my fellow sitters in this séance. They all had perplexed expressions. Gwenn tilted her head toward me to keep talking. She'd relinquished her role as the medium. It was up to me to keep the line open to Reggie and get him to focus on what we needed from him.

I opened my mouth to repeat the questions but was interrupted by a singing Reggie.

"You know that tune? Right? It's from my old pirate days. I loved that song almost as much as the rum we sang about. Songs told stories, Alex. They communicated what our life was like. There was magic in them there words. There was friendship."

"Yeah. I understand about friendship," I said. "I value

the friendship with you, Reggie. I'm forever grateful that you took on the role I handed to you."

A wispy sigh came out of the crystal. "There's more magic. Find the ship's treasure map, and it will guide you."

I sensed the heightened awareness of the group. Sebastian had the map. They'd been denied access to the secrets it protected. "We have the it but it's no use to us. There's a curse on it."

Laughter erupted and poured from the crystal. "Didn't you hear me? I said there's magic in them words. Recite them to the map."

"I don't have it with me. I can get it, but then what? How do I use it to open a portal to the Underworld? I have to reach Prince Jasper and strike a deal with him. I need the weapons his smithy made."

"Wart's gone. The prince don't have a smithy no more. I heard tell he has a cache of weapons that one of his demon dogs guards. None of us go near it. Not worth the trouble."

"I just need to talk to Jasper. Do you think you can get a message to him for me?"

"Sorry. I've been lying low since he began his siege on our route. I can't go near him. I'll see what I can do to relay that you want to parley." The crystal grew cloudy. Reggie's voice grew distant. "Remember to sing. Good luck."

A loud crack resounded in the center of the table like a snap of electricity. Every candle flame extinguished.

"Damn," Nick said.

"Indeed," Gwenn said. "I've never encountered anything like it."

My heart raced. I had to get the map, which was at Sebastian's. Janda was also at Sebastian's. I was screwed. I banged my head repeatedly on the table. "Why me? There's no way to sneak past my wife. She's too damn good."

Mutther chuckled. "That's what you get for falling for one of the best Sleepy Hollow hunters to exist. But not to worry. We also happen to have one of the best witches in Sleepy Hollow." He grinned at Gwenn. "Right, dear?"

She pursed her lips. "Aren't you all a great bunch? Putting me in the hot seat. Thanks a lot."

I took hold of her hand. "Please? This is for Janda's sake. Hell. It's for all our sakes. If I can't bring back weapons to turn the tide of the ghost apocalypse, then we are all in serious trouble."

"Oh, good grief. Stop looking at me like that." She gazed around the group. "Alex has a valid point, so fine, I'll do it."

I released her hand and gave her my *you're the best* smile. "Thanks."

She stood and took a deep breath, then another. "The air is filled with spiritual energy. Much of it is good, seeking to move forward. Some of it is evil, seeking a way out. The horseman has a human on his side. The first step is for Alex to update everyone on what his tech guy discovered." She grabbed her purse and dug out her car keys. "You can do that while I take the herbs to Janda. One of you will have to create a distraction long enough for me to get the map."

Sebastian was already on his feet. "Thank you for doing this. I would go, but it would be difficult for me to leave Janda to get the map to Alex. You have the best chance of success. It's on my desk. If she catches you in the study, use Hulda's journal as a reason for being there." He pivoted to face Alex. "I'm the fastest here. As soon as you fill the rest of us in, I'll head home and create a stir by making demands on Damon regarding the shifter patrols. Of course, I'll have to apologize later." He paused. "Or not."

Gwenn picked up Hudson and stuffed him in his carrier.

"Time to visit Auntie Janda." The cat purred. "I'll be back as soon as I can. When are you trying to do this map thing?"

"Tonight." My nerves were strung tight. The sooner I started, the better.

"All righty, then." Hudson meowed. Gwenn closed the carrier. "Yes, Hudson, it sounds like it will be an interesting night, especially after the séance which has undoubtedly gotten the attention of the ghosts in the area."

As soon as she drove off, Nick started for the kitchen. "Great. More ghosts. I hope there's something to eat, or it's going to be a shitty night."

"Gwenn has chocolate chip cookies," I said. "And lemonade."

Nick frowned. "Just my luck. Better than nothing. I'll be right back."

Everyone except for Sebastian devoured the cookies while I told them about Sid's discovery. Cusses, hisses, and growls interrupted me several times. I didn't blame them. It sucked no matter how you looked at it. Evening was creeping in faster than I'd like, which meant I was running out of time before I'd have to go check on Janda. It also meant we were approaching the peak hours of the ghost attacks.

Sebastian pulled on a new cape. This one, he said, was untainted by my ass.

"I may not make it back for when you pry the secrets from the map," he said. "If not, I wish you well, Alex. Never fear for Janda and the baby. Nothing will harm them."

He was gone before I could thank him. Like me, Sebastian was a different person after Janda entered our lives. That in itself was all the thanks either of us desired.

"Now all we have to do is wait," Mutther said.

I pulled back the curtain and stared out at the looming sunset. "Now we wait."

CHAPTER II
YO-HO-HO

" Stop the pacing. You're driving me nuts," Nick said.

"Shut up. It helps me think." I strode back across the length of the parlor, pausing again to see if Gwenn's car was coming down the street.

It had taken months to restore the upper level of the historical society building that had burned when the Headless Horseman had organized the attack to recover his sword. The damage had been extensive, but the town bounced back and worked together to rebuild the structure that held so much history. Fresh paint coated all the walls, and the smell of ash had finally dissipated.

On my sixth pass around the room, I heard a car pull up outside. I froze. Nick halted his complaining, and Mutther dashed out to meet Gwenn. Hudson trotted in front of them as they came inside.

"How did it go?" I'd heard nothing from either Gwenn or Sebastian the whole time. My muscles had started doing that involuntary twitching thing. Tense didn't begin to describe how I felt.

Gwenn held up the piece of parchment. "Here you go."

I let out a breath. "Thanks."

"Don't thank me until we can get past the curse on this map. I, for one, am not keen on a repeat of experiencing the jolt it gave me the last time I attempted to get it to reveal its secrets." She moved all the candles out of the way and spread the map out on the table.

My phone vibrated. It was our police friend, Shawn. I'd contacted him to share most of what Sid had discovered about Stephan Turner. The police needed to know that they might confront a half-demon, a threat we knew little about. "Hey, Shawn, I'm with the others. I'm putting you on speaker. Is that okay?"

"Sure," Shawn said. "Hi, everyone. I have a bit of news to pass along. It seems Sid was spot-on about Turner. The guy is nuts. He's also the one who founded the prankster forum. At this point, there's not a damn thing we can charge him with. Nothing points to him doing anything illegal. We also released two of the suspects arrested during the bagel shop incident. They were clean. No records. Just stupid as far as I could tell. They got an official warning. My understanding is they got out of Sleepy Hollow fast. I suppose meeting an actual vampire and shifters will do that to some folks." He chuckled. "Seriously, though, I wish I had more to share. The other guy is refusing to talk. We have him on assault, but the judge will be setting bail, so we'll be forced to cut him loose."

We grumbled our displeasure, but Shawn cut us off. "That doesn't mean we won't have detectives tailing him. We're just as interested as you are to follow this to its source. I'm doing what I can. Just wanted to give you an update."

"We appreciate it," I said. "I get that you have to follow the letter of the law. You're a good cop. I owe you one."

"You owe me nothing. It's my job. Catch you later," Shawn said.

While I had my phone out, I sent a heart emoji to Janda. She sent back an animated cartoon image of her blowing a kiss.

Sebastian rushed into the room from the rear entrance, saw we hadn't started yet, and relaxed. "That wife of yours sure knows how to waylay my plans. I only made it out because I said I would bring back ice cream."

"Welcome to my world." I could cross getting ice cream off my list. "How was the ghost traffic on the way over?"

He shrugged. "Minimal. That won't last once the sun has gone down."

Nick grunted. "Sucks at night anymore." He pulled out a chair and plunked himself down. "Let's get this serenade rolling."

I glanced at the map. "Reggie said to sing to it. I wonder if we have to do anything special."

Nick screwed up his face. "Like what?"

"How the hell should I know? Never mind. Does anyone know the words to the song Reggie mentioned?" My mind had gone blank. Singing a song to a map seemed ridiculous, but I'd try anything.

"I only remember about the rum," Nick said.

Gwenn rolled her eyes at him and scrolled down her phone to show us what she'd found. "If this is the correct version, then we repeat the words and hope the curse will back off."

The map lay dormant on the table—an old piece of parchment depicting the topography of a different era. I held a tiny shred of hope this would work. I'd seen plenty of supernatural shit to know anything was possible, even singing to a damn map. If it didn't divulge its secrets, then

I'd have no other option than Stephan Turner. I did *not* want to involve that lunatic if I could avoid it.

Gwenn played the tune on her phone, and the rest of us belted out the words, and at the chorus of 'yo-ho-ho, a pirate's life for me', the map freaking lit up. It glowed like Mutther's neon bar sign. Gwenn motioned for us to continue. We kept going. I was too afraid to stop now.

A burst of light exploded from the map.

"Holy Mother!" Nick yelled. "What the hell?"

We stopped singing and watched an entire layer of the map disappear. It actually went totally blank. A moment later, dark lines crisscrossed over the surface. The lines became images, and the images became a whole new map.

I sucked in my breath because I'd seen this depiction in-person. "Sweet Jesus." I glanced from the map to my friends. "It's the Underworld."

"Are you sure?" Mutther said.

"I not only saw this place," I said, "but lived there. I built a safe house in the area around those boulders." I pointed to a stretch of rocky hillside. It was the same hillside Janda and I had traversed and where she had fallen down the deep crevice to land on me.

"But what does this mean?" Gwenn said. She trailed her finger along a bold line that indicated a path through the boulders.

"Hold on," Sebastian said. "Gwenn, do you have one of the old topography maps of Sleepy Hollow?"

"Somewhere. I'll look." She ran off to dig through one of the boxes she'd yet to sort.

Sebastian's eyes glistened with excitement. "I think I know what this is."

Gwenn returned with the map and handed it to Sebastian. He placed it next to the one of the Underworld.

"Take a close look at this thick line on the Underworld map." He pointed to where he meant. "Now look at the map of Sleepy Hollow."

"I'll be damned," Mutther said. "It follows the same path as the aqueduct trail, but how? The aqueduct couldn't have been there when this map was made, right?"

"It doesn't matter whether the chicken or the egg came first," Sebastian said. "What matters is knowing the maps mirror one another."

I saw where he was going with his theory. "Which means we can combine them to find the similarities and use that to discover where the two planes meet. That juncture should be the entrance to the Underworld."

I collapsed into a chair, stunned by what we'd learned. I could do this. I could at least enter the Underworld. Getting out might not be so easy, but this was huge. This was the break we needed.

My phone sent me an intrusion alert. "Dammit! Let's go. Janda's in trouble." I rolled up the map and shoved it at Gwenn. "Don't let this out of your sight. Nick, guard Gwenn."

I tore out the back door and shifted. Mutther took to the skies. Nick stayed to protect Gwenn and the map. Sebastian was already gone.

CHAPTER 12

BATTLE CRY

When ghosts congregated, an odd effect occurred. They became more visible. They also hummed. It wasn't like Reggie when he hummed a few bars of the pirate song. It was akin to a hive of bees discussing where to find a source of pollen. In their own way, they communicated with one another. As living entities, we caught a fraction of the conversation. What I heard as I drew nearer to them made my blood run cold.

"They say her child will be a powerful beacon. The prince's son will use that magic."

The words buzzed in the air as the message passed from one apparition to the next. It became more garbled when it filtered through the ranks to the less populated sections until I could no longer hear it.

A stream of fire hit the front line of the gathering. The ghosts scattered. Mutther dove from above, spewing flames across their ranks.

"Fall back," some said. "It's not time."

The hive message trickled through the gathering, and

the ghostly congregation split apart. I chased a small group of five or six—at least it seemed like that many. The energy manifested by their proximity to one another dwindled, the chill in the night air dissipated, and the temperature rose to normal levels. They had departed, and not in the "dearly departed soul" kind of way. They were there one moment and gone the next.

One thing remained long after they left. It was the words that stirred them into action and had become their battle cry—*the baby.*

They wanted my daughter.

Sebastian stood a hundred yards or so in front of his house, just on the outside of the barrier. Even if the ghosts couldn't find the house, they'd eventually come upon Sebastian. I'd never seen him so damn scary looking. You'd be a fool to mess with an ancient vampire protecting his own. If our intel was correct, Stephan Turner seemed to be the force behind the attacks. It made me wonder which entity the ghosts truly followed—the horseman, who may have thought he was manipulating Turner, or Turner, who seemed to have the upper hand. Either way, it was bad for the rest of us.

Mutther landed near Sebastian and shifted. I bounded up in my panther form.

"They're gone, Alex," Mutther said. "You can stand down."

That was easy for him to say. He had gained complete mastery over his dragon. My panther was not so docile. It didn't want to stand down. I hissed and growled, agreeing with my panther. I had to protect my family.

"Listen to him, Alex. Save your energy. You have a long road to travel, still. Stand down." Sebastian met my gaze and held it.

I huffed but shifted. "Could you hear them? They want the baby!" Breathing was hard. My chest heaved, and my muscles twitched like mad.

Mutther put a hand on my shoulder. "That will never happen. You have my word as a Pendragon. I will protect Janda and the baby with my life."

I tried to smile, but my mouth wouldn't cooperate. I settled for a grunt. Mutther understood and nodded before jogging far enough away from the house so he could shift safely into his dragon. He was careful to fly in random locations on the chance our enemies might be watching.

Once the dragon disappeared in the distance, Sebastian started back to the house but paused. "Are you sure you want to risk going to the Underworld?"

I glared at him. He had to be off his rocker. The Underworld was my only chance to save my family. "You know I have to go."

He stared out over the treetops for a moment. "I know you think you have to go because you don't know what else to do. I've been around many battles in my day, but nothing like this. Bringing weapons back will be near impossible. Even if you get the cooperation of the demon prince, will his weapons be enough?"

"I don't know." My shoulders sagged. Exhaustion and doubt crept in. "I'll set out at daybreak when the ghosts are less likely to be around to interfere."

There was pity in Sebastian's eyes. "Then you better spend the night with Janda and hold her as if you will never see her again because you may not return. I wish you wouldn't make the same mistakes I made with Hulda. But I understand the torment you're enduring. I truly do."

He left me standing at the boundary of his home, where Hulda's spell had yet to be fully tested. We'd cut off the attack before they could breach the protective barrier. The assaults were testing our line of defense and prodding to find where Janda might be hidden. They were getting closer. It wouldn't be long before they knew for sure where she was located. It was good that Janda had moved in with Sebastian. Every layer of security mattered.

The walk through the barrier seemed harder than before. Gwenn must have added extra protections to it. I'd have to thank her the next time I saw her. A turmoil of emotions gripped me as I stepped farther into its depths. Whether they were caused by my current state of despair or the additional spells that had been cast, I didn't know. I wanted to cry one second and laugh the next. It was odd. I pressed onward. Other feelings stirred, like anger and frustration. Right as I passed through the last of the barrier and laid eyes on the house where Janda waited, one emotion rose to the top—love.

I inhaled and let the warmth of that feeling wash over me and comfort me. Sebastian had placed a bin of clothes near a tree for anyone who would need it. I slipped into a casual jogging suit and went to the rear entrance by the garage.

Tomorrow was the start of September. I was leaving my pregnant wife just days before her estimated due date. It killed me to not share my plans with her. I could only hope she'd forgive me. Tonight, I'd pamper her and help her come up with a name for the baby. I wanted to know our daughter's name before I left.

CHAPTER 13

RECLINERS ROCK

My wife was relaxing in the new massage recliner I'd bought her as a surprise. She seemed unaware of the latest attempt the ghosts had made to reach her.

"Oh. My. God. Alex, this is heaven. You have to try it." She pushed her way out of the recliner and tugged on me until I relented and got into it. "Well? Is this the best thing since toasters were made or what?"

I grinned. "I think you mean since sliced bread." The chair did feel pretty incredible.

She scoffed at me. "In my world, it's toasters. You can only do so much with sliced bread, but a toaster? That's perfection. All sorts of goodness comes from a toaster." She paused a moment then blurted out, "Pop Tarts! I mean, who the hell doesn't love Pop Tarts? Or bagels? The world changed for the better when we discovered toasted bagels."

She furrowed her brows. The little kitchenette that Sebastian had installed was filled with a myriad of treats. She began digging around in the cabinets.

69

"I'm positive George sent over fresh bagels today." She held up a bakery bag in triumph. "Ah-ha! See? Bagels. Do you want one? I'm going to have an everything bagel smothered in cream cheese."

"No, thanks." I closed my eyes. "I'm fine." I sank deeper into the seat cushion. "Holy smokes. This massage recliner *is* awesome. It even has a butt warmer. I'm glad I got it for you." I opened my eyes and winked at her.

She laughed, and my heart nearly broke.

The aroma of toasted onion from the bagel had my stomach rumbling. It was a tough choice, but I relinquished my cozy spot and went to the kitchenette. "Changed my mind." I sliced an everything bagel in half and popped it into the toaster. "I'll make some coffee and spread cream cheese on your bagel when it's ready. You can go back to your chair. Thanks for sharing it." I kissed the top of her head and set to work preparing a tray to bring to her.

She settled back into the recliner and began playing with the massage settings. "Oh!" Her eyes grew enormous. "This setting has my lady bits tingling, if you know what I mean. Wow."

I got our bagels and coffee together, brought over the tray, and put it next to her on a small table. "Damn. If I'd known it would do that, then I'd have bought it sooner."

"You should definitely give this setting a go. Oh, boy. Wowsers." She was enjoying the sensation.

I came up behind her and began a gentle neck massage. I slid my hand lower beneath her shirt to cup her breasts and slide my thumb over her nipples.

She closed her eyes and arched into the caress. "Keep going, and I may have to find a new use for this recliner."

I exhaled as my cock hardened. "I'm game to give it a go." I helped her out of her clothes and eased her back into the recliner, then stripped in front of her and began stroking my cock. "How's the chair now?"

Her eyes glistened with desire while gooseflesh covered her arms. She was getting into the provocative teasing. I kneeled before her and ran my fingers along her moist clit. I increased the vibration of the massage settings then explored her with my tongue.

"Oh! Alex!" She gasped in delight. Sex had not been on our radar of late, but this massage chair was a game changer. I wanted her to know she would always be sexy to me, even when she didn't feel attractive.

I stood by the side of the recliner and let her watch me run my hands up and down my shaft. She moaned and cranked up the vibration knob to its highest setting. I bent over, still stroking myself, and suckled her breasts. My plan to seduce my wife got sidetracked when she guided my cock closer to her lips. My breath caught as she took me in her mouth, teasing me with her tongue. I pushed my fingers into the wetness of her clit and rubbed her, matching the movements of her mouth over my cock. In and out. She climaxed with an intense shudder that sent me over the edge and continued until I spilled my seed.

I propped my arms against the top of the chair while holding my body far enough away from her to keep from putting my weight on her belly. We gazed at one another. Neither of us could speak. The massage chair continued to vibrate. I reached down and reduced the setting on it then kneeled by her side.

"This is one hell of a good chair," she said. Her voice was lazy with contentment.

"My thoughts exactly." I was so lucky to have this amazing woman as my mate.

As soon as my legs would cooperate, I stood, kissed her,

and reheated our coffee. I moved the ottoman next to the recliner and ate my everything bagel with the person who was everything to me.

"What's on your mind?" she said.

"What do you mean?"

She pushed the buttons on her recliner so the massage stopped, the footrest went to its folded-in position, and the back was upright. She sat on the edge and gazed intently at me. "You have worry written all over your face. That's what I mean. You should stop trying to fix the world, Alex. Some things are not yours to fix."

"I can't stop," I said. "You and the baby are my entire existence."

She brushed my cheek with her hand. "There are many times where I sit and wonder how the universe could have thought I was a good match for you. Then I stopped wondering and leaned into your love. That's all I want, no matter what happens."

"Thank you," I said. It didn't begin to describe how I felt.

"You're welcome." She rose a bit ungracefully but recovered and went off to retrieve a small notebook she'd been writing in earlier. She grabbed an afghan and wrapped it around her body before flipping open the notebook and striding around the room. "Now as to naming our baby, I started a list."

"Funny you should mention it because I have a list as well. It's in my head." I tapped my forehead. "You start."

"Adelaide, Belladonna, Callistra." She paused. "I went through the entire alphabet, so sit back and relax. It's gonna take a while."

I stifled a laugh. "The floor is all yours."

At one point, Janda gave up striding around the room

and eased into the recliner. We were on U, and admittedly, neither of us were impressed with Ursula. She crossed that one out and wrote Una, pronounced with the long double o sound. We thought that one would be confusing to pronounce and ended up crossing it off the list. Violetta was an intriguing option that we starred for future reference.

"Okay," she said. "Next up is Wrenley."

"Stop," I said. "That's the one. Wrens are good luck. Plus, they're feisty and intelligent, which is how I picture our daughter. It's how I see you."

Janda gave me an air kiss. "Wrenley is a glorious name. It was one of my top picks."

"How about Wrenley Maeve?"

"Wrenley Maeve Holden. I like that a lot. Our daughter is lucky to have you for a father." Janda yawned.

I tucked the afghan around her. "You should rest."

Her eyes closed. I got dressed as quietly as possible and almost made it out the door.

"Off again? You don't fool me, Alexander Holden." She gazed at me through half-opened lids.

I froze with my hand on the doorknob. "Really?" I turned and grinned. "I must be slipping."

She shook her head. "Nah. You didn't say anything when you came in, but you don't have much of a poker face. I assumed more ghosts were trying to come knocking and you were letting them know they had the wrong house. Besides, you all were loud out there."

"Sorry. They're persistent creatures. I wish I knew how to get them to stop." I didn't dare let slip where I was going in search of those answers.

She closed her eyes and mumbled. "You'll figure it out. Just be careful. Wrenley and I want you here for her arrival, and in one piece." She yawned again. "Maybe we should put up one of those signs that says *No Soliciting*."

"If only it was that simple," I said. "It might work if Gwenn developed repellent paint we could use on the sign."

Janda didn't respond. She had dozed off. I tiptoed over and kissed her. Then I left.

CHAPTER 14

CROSSROADS

Night in the woods around Sleepy Hollow could be interesting at any time of the year. We were now officially into September, and that meant more tourists would find their way into town before the full schedule of Spooktacular October events began. A few ghost-seekers who had heard about an uptick in supernatural activity had started poking around.

Mostly, they found nothing. Not that there wasn't shit happening, but these were amateurs who had zero clue where to locate an apparition. The police let them investigate old abandoned buildings that Angie had "accidentally" let slip were haunted. It was a surprise to us when once or twice a ghost actually showed up. So far, we'd avoided any real catastrophe. The encounters had been innocuous. No Headless Horseman recruits wandered into the areas Angie had pointed out to the ghost enthusiasts.

The spot where Nick and I were to meet was quiet for now. This sector had seen a rise in paranormal energy that had me looking over my shoulder numerous times on my way here. I had shifted into my panther and raced the entire distance to the rendezvous point. This time, I came prepared. We'd devised an awkward but somewhat effective method for carrying around a change of clothes. We strapped a pair of sweats and a tee to our leg. The only time it could become a problem would be if humans saw an animal with a bundle tied to its leg. We decided to risk it. If a naked human was seen running through the woods or along alleyways, it would likely cause more commotion than an animal moving so fast that folks would question what they had witnessed.

In the middle of pulling on my pants, I detected movement. I hovered on the point of shifting into my panther but waited, flaring my nostrils and testing the air for hostile scents. Nick pushed his way through some shrubbery. I relaxed and finished putting on my clothes as he trotted forward.

"You have it?" I said.

He shifted back. "What do you think?" He untied his bundle and pulled out the map. "Here you go. I sure as hell hope this works."

"Yeah. Me, too."

I opened the map while Nick dressed. In the moonlight, I could just barely detect the lines that indicated the path we had to follow. We knew roughly where the juncture should exist. Interestingly, it was in the heart of the Sleepy Hollow forest, just a few miles east of the prison for supernaturals. I'd expected it to be along the river somewhere, in the general region of where Janda had found the pirate treasure. I was wrong. Reggie had said the map would guide us, so here we were staring blankly from the map to the ground to each other.

"I don't see a blasted thing that looks like an entrance," Nick said.

The spot where were should have found an entrance to the Underworld defied logic. There was nothing out of place in the landscape.

"Shit." I huffed my annoyance and surveyed our surroundings.

Nick began kicking tree trunks. "Maybe it's hidden inside a tree."

"What are you two doing?" Sebastian said, appearing as if a ghost himself.

I spun around. "You enjoy that, don't you? Janda always said you did."

He shrugged. "At my age, you take joy in the simple things in life." He glanced at the map. "This isn't promising."

"No kidding," I said. "What the hell do we do now?"

Nick grabbed a stick and stabbed the ground and surrounding bushes. "That map is old. The land has changed too much to find anything. I give up." He tossed the stick at a cluster of rocks.

Woof!

We all froze. I tipped my head toward where the bark had come from and motioned for us to approach slowly. I took two steps forward when a dog popped its head up from between the rocks and barked at me in a non-menacing way.

"Hey, fella. Are you lost?" I reached out with my hand, palm up and low to let it know I wasn't a threat.

The dog hopped up on a rock so it was now eye-level with me. I paused.

"That's not a *he*," Nick said. "But she seems friendly enough."

The dog was young. She wasn't a puppy yet not full-grown either. She was brown with some variegation to the tone. Her ears seemed too big for her head and were pointed in alertness. She was hairless.

Nick came closer. "Is that one of those Mexican hairless breeds?"

The dog watched us from her vantage point. She made no move to jump down or to attack.

"Hmm," Sebastian said. "If I'm not mistaken, this is a guard dog." He stayed where he was—well out of reach of the dog's sharp teeth.

"Guard dog?" I said. "Guarding what?"

Sebastian took a step back. "The Underworld. She may look innocent, but don't be fooled. That dog is a trained killer. She's adept at destroying the supernatural." He took another step back. "I, for one, will be staying away from her."

The dog jumped back between the rocks. A few seconds later, she emerged holding a pirate's hat.

"Holy shit," I said. "Reggie's hat."

Wisps of steam rose from the folds of the fabric, sending a hefty aroma of sulfur in our direction.

Nick fanned his nose and squinted. "That's nasty."

I glanced over at him. "That's the Underworld."

"No, thanks," Nick said.

I chuckled. "You get used to it."

Now that we knew the dog must have been sent by Reggie, we gathered closer. Nick attempted to take the hat from the dog.

She growled.

"She's a bit possessive," Nick said, retreating. "I hear ya, girl. That's a nice doggie. Pretty collar you're wearing. I'm backing up now. You can keep Reggie's smelly hat."

Sebastian nudged me forward. "You try to take it."

"Why? So she can eat me and not you?" I was plenty skeptical about that bit of advice. "Not a fan of that idea."

Sebastian shoved me closer. "You can be so ignorant at times, Alex. Just take the hat. She's obviously here for you."

I glared at Sebastian. "Sure, she is."

I noticed the amber-colored stone collar Nick pointed out. If I was right, it was made from brimstone. Whether the demon prince infused the stones with magic was something I didn't want to find out the hard way.

I glanced over at Nick. "And what happens if she attacks? Are you going to pull her off of me?"

"Not me," Nick said. "Sorry, bud. You're on your own." He took a few more steps backward until he stood beside Sebastian.

"Thanks. I'm glad you two have my back." I did my best not to stare directly at the dog. A perceived challenge would not have a good outcome. I took a breath and touched the hat without trying to take it. "Easy, girl. I'm a friend of Reggie's."

She dropped the hat.

"Okay," I said. I bent down to pick it up while keeping one eye on her. She didn't move. I took the hat back to Nick and Sebastian. "I have the hat, but now what?"

"I'm not sure," Sebastian said.

The three of us were in the middle of the woods in the pre-dawn hours with a guard dog from the Underworld. Life continued to send us strange crap to deal with. The Headless Horseman, a parade of ghosts, and now a supernatural attack dog. I didn't want to know what else would come our way.

One thing at a time. Get to the Underworld and figure out the rest later.

I held that thought front and center while we debated our options.

"It's clear that this dog is your guide to the Underworld," Sebastian said. "Unfortunately, I'm at a loss as to how to prompt the dog to lead the way."

A chill hit the air hard. We stopped talking and strained our senses.

Pop! Pop! Pop!

Several ghosts appeared at the edge of the trees to our left. Their violent intent was unmistakable when they rushed at us with raised fists.

The dog barked, then jumped in front of me, gnashing her teeth and growling like a banshee. The ghosts didn't heed the warning. Too bad for them. The dog went nuts. She bit into one ghost and tore off its leg. I had no idea something could do that to an apparition. She didn't stop there. She tore into them in a blaze of fury—literally.

Flames shot out of her mouth and sulfurous smoke from her nostrils. Her eyes had gone fiery orange. The collar around her neck lit up. Yeah. Definitely a magical collar.

"Jumping Jesus," Nick said. "Will you look at that?"

"Hard not to," I said. "She's something else."

"She's a supernatural guard dog," Sebastian said.

All the apparitions had been dispatched in quick fashion, and we stood in utter astonishment at this incredible dog. We'd discovered the crossroads the hidden layer of the map had revealed and had found my guide to the Underworld. My journey was about to begin.

CHAPTER 15

DOWN THE RABBIT HOLE

This was akin to Alice going down the rabbit hole. That was all I could think of as I paused on top of the boulder where the dog had stood moments earlier before she disappeared down a gap in the stones. She'd dispensed with the ghosts in quick fashion and had hopped back to her spot on the rock. The collar had gone dark. Her eyes had turned brown once more. I was grateful the flames and smoke had also ceased.

"Keep Janda safe," I said to the others. That was the one thing that tore at me. I wanted to be by my wife's side. I also wanted to stop the invasion of ghosts the horseman had set loose. Thanks to the dog shredding those apparitions, I knew it was possible. All I needed was a supernatural weapon.

"Without question," Sebastian replied.

Nick nodded agreement. "Safe journey, my friend."

I waved and slipped into the hole and the darkness below. I began counting in my head to see how long it took to reach the bottom. *One. Two. Three. Four—*

"Dammit."

I hit the rough stone side of the tunnel and lost count. I was barefoot, so when I hit the bottom, the landing stung with a force that jolted up my calves. I sat splayed out on my ass, staring up at a faint light above. Dawn had arrived. The dog came up and licked my face.

"How did you ever get up there?" Returning the way I'd come was out of the question. "If I make it out of here, I need you to show me a better path back home."

She barked once.

"I'm holding you to that." I ran my hand down her back. She wagged her tail. I rose and brushed dirt from my clothes to give my eyes time to adjust to the darkness. "Okay. I'm ready. Lead the way."

She bounded off.

"Wait." I jogged after her, feeling each pebble and the unevenness of the terrain with my bare feet. I caught up and almost plowed into her when she halted. She crouched low to the earth. I followed her example and sank to the ground. She glanced my way before crawling forward. I got the message. Stealth.

We passed a group of unnaturals roaming like the zombies they were down here. Unnaturals were people who had gotten off-course, so to speak—spirits who had gotten stuck or lost. Whenever living people like myself ended up in the Underworld, the unnaturals were drawn to us like moths to a flame. I'd learned that the last time I was in the Underworld. I suppose I was one of them back then, but not quite. I had an anchor in the living world that set me apart from them. I had Janda. She saved me, body and soul. I only escaped with her help as a gifted traveler. I did *not* want to think of how she'd respond when she discovered I'd come back to this God-forsaken place. She would kill me.

The unnaturals meandered past our hiding spot without noticing my presence. I breathed a sigh of relief. My guide dog bounced up from her crouched position and trotted down the pathway. I followed. We were still in a tunnel, but now and then, I noticed a break above us that allowed a modicum of light to filter down to us. The Underworld was always dark. It had shades of grays that I suppose mimicked the natural daily cycle in the living realm. Time also meant little here. Janda and I had found that out when we spent what we thought was one night in my hidden quarters only to discover she'd been gone for over two months.

The dog ascended a slope. The angle became steeper as I climbed upward. I lost sight of her. She was quick and knew the terrain. She didn't return, so I assumed I was on my own. The path became narrower until I had to stoop and crawl the rest of the way out. I emerged in an area I recognized. I was standing in the wasteland of burned trees that surrounded the area where I'd made my hidden refuge. I couldn't have been too far from it. I scanned my surroundings for the dog. There was no trace of her.

All that was left was to begin the trek toward the Underworld town. The surface was warmer here than in the underground path. My feet ached from the journey, and I was sure I had one or two blisters. It didn't matter as long as I got what I came for. I continued toward town and stopped only to avoid detection by unnaturals. My pace quickened on the main road. I had to see Maude. She was the only one who could help me with setting up a meeting with the demon prince.

As soon as I reached the town boundary, I made a beeline for Maude's place. I knocked on the door.

The familiar woman who wore layers of ragged clothes

and a funky hat opened the door and grinned. "Welcome back."

Under normal conditions, in the realm of the living, I'd respond with a line about how it was good to be back. Not in this case. I didn't want to be here, but I smiled at her anyway. "Thanks. Can I see Maude?"

She shut the door, and we walked into the main part of the bar, where all manner of folks mingled. The dead who'd accepted their fate joked and drank. Then they drank some more. A few raised their glasses of murky booze as I passed by. I nodded.

The commotion of my presence must have alerted Maude. She came lumbering out of her office, all smiles, and grabbed me in a bear hug that took my breath away.

"Ack. It's good to see you, boy." She poked me with her finger. "I see you're still alive. Pity. I was hoping you'd stick around to give Reggie a hand as our ferryman. Times been tough since you left, but we get by."

I lowered my voice to keep the busybodies from overhearing me. "I require a meeting with Jasper. Can you do that?"

Her eyebrows nearly touched her hairline. "What in tarnation would you want to do that for? Have you lost your marbles?"

"Maybe. I'm here, so that's one indicator I've lost my mind."

She let out one of her deep belly laughs. "Oh, how I missed you." She smacked my back. "Come on. Let's go into my office."

She lifted a hand to catch the eye of the barkeep. He nodded and went off to the back room, where I knew he kept a private stash just for Maude.

We entered her office, and she closed the door, muting the hum of activity in the bar.

She scrutinized me as she took a seat behind her desk. "You ain't wearing shoes." She made a note of it on a piece of paper. She'd get me a pair before I left. Then I'd owe her a favor. That's how things worked with the leader of the Underworld black market.

I wasn't sure what the price would be to set up a meeting with the demon prince.

CHAPTER 16

A ROYAL PAIN

The meeting with Maude ended with me wearing a pair of sneakers that would cost me nothing—or so she said. According to her, I'd already done enough while doing my stint as her underground ferryman. But since she was going to pull in a favor to get my audience with Prince Jasper, she had one thing to ask of me. If I ever found myself in the position to help reopen an underground route, then it would be much appreciated. So, that was the true cost of her getting the message to the demon prince that I wanted to see him. I told her I'd do my best with the route.

I didn't go back to the tiny apartment I'd once occupied. I was sure someone else would be using it. I also knew from Janda that its location had been compromised when she and Wart stopped there when she was here before. It was hard to imagine that almost a year had gone by since then. Wart had been a kind of viewing box for the prince, who could see whatever went on around his smithy, whom he'd sent off to assist Janda. I hung around the alleys like I'd told Maude I would and waited for word from her.

Reggie found me. He was grinning from ear-to-ear. "So good to see ya, mate. Did ya bring me cap?"

"Good to see you, too." I pulled the crumpled hat from beneath my shirt. It'd been hard to carry it around in the tunnels, so the best option was to stuff it inside my shirt. "Here you go." I handed it to him.

"Thanks, mate. I been missing this old thing. It has a habit of getting misplaced but seems to always show up when I wants it. Imagine that." His toothless grin widened.

"I'm imagining it as we speak." His pirate hat had certainly gotten around through the centuries. I wondered if it had picked up a touch of magic along the way and that was why it always ended up returning to its owner. "Did you bring news from Maude for me?"

Reggie fiddled with his hat, smoothing out the wrinkles and shoving it on his head. "Oh, yeah. Right. I has it here somewhere." He searched his pants and then his shirt. There was a slight crinkling of paper when he patted his chest. His eyes brightened, and he wiggled his brows. "Always keep what's important close to ya chest, if you knows what I means."

"That I do." My patience grew thin as I waited.

He found the paper and held it out. "Here ya go, mate. Follow them directions, and you'll find the demon prince." He furrowed his brows. "Are you sure you wants to go near the demon prince? It ain't a good idea to stir up the hornet's nest, ya know."

I took the paper that was a hand-drawn map. What was with all these maps?

"Thanks, Reggie. I'm aware the demon is someone not to be trusted. If there was another way, I'd take it. Tell Maude thanks." A thought hit me. "You wouldn't happen to know if there's a hidden layer on this map, would you?"

He seemed puzzled by the question. "It's not a pirate map. It's just a map, ain't it? It shows you how to get around or how to find somethin' as far as I know." He stabbed a crooked finger at the paper. "That spot there is where ya want to go. These lines here show you the way." He pointed to the paths drawn on the map.

"Right you are," I said, tucking the map under my shirt the same way Reggie had done. If there was something hidden beneath the surface of the map, it eluded me. Reggie sure didn't think there was anything hidden, so I took it at face value and said my goodbyes.

He lifted his pirate hat, waved it at me, then stuck it back on his head. "I see that worried look on your face. I'm doing fine. Being the ferryman is sorta fun. Keeps me busy. Idle hands be the devil's workshop. Ain't nothing idle about my hands."

He nodded then walked off at a casual stroll, his hands in his pockets, and whistled a jaunty tune. It was a stark contrast to the gloom of the Underworld. It was a buoy of hope in a dark land. Maybe this idiotic plan of mine would work after all.

I followed the directions on the map. I walked and walked. Out of town, down the road leading through the woods, slipping out of sight when unnaturals drew too close, then coming out of hiding and walking some more. For the love of all things holy, why were there no modes of transportation in the Underworld? Other than the rare boat to cross the river, there was nothing. Not a car, truck, motorcycle, plane, helicopter, or even a bike. Although, I had heard someone talk about a bike once. Just never saw one the entire time I lived here. I suppose it didn't matter to most people here. They had all the time in the world to get where they were going. They had eternity.

It was the smell of sulfur that cued me to the presence I sought. I paused. The dog that guided me trotted up and rubbed against my leg.

"I see you've met my friend Sasha." Jasper, son of the devil and prince of this area of the Underworld, stepped away from the tree he'd been leaning against.

"Yes. She's quite the dog. I didn't realize she belonged to you." I kept my posture straight but with an air of indifference to the demon prince's presence. It wouldn't help my cause to appear desperate for his aid. He would extract a high price for his services, and I had to be careful what I agreed to do in return.

Jasper ambled over and snapped his fingers at Sasha. She instantly heeled at his side. Jasper patted Sasha's head as he spoke. "I'm told you want to see me." He shrugged. "I'm easy to find if you know where to look."

I smiled. "I discovered the tunnel leading to your brimstone lava pits had an unfortunate cave-in. I resorted to asking for a meeting, since your front door was permanently shut."

"Yes. It's quite unfortunate about the tunnel collapse. I heard how certain routes have met a similar demise. A shame. Wouldn't you say?" The orange-red glint in his eyes showed the true nature of his origins. He was a product of Hell.

The underlying message was obvious. Jasper had found the underground route and shut it down. He had to know I'd used that route to ferry souls out that didn't belong here. I kept my face blank.

"It sounds like a lot has happened during my absence."

"Indeed," Jasper said. His red horns glowed slightly before dimming. He brushed back his long dark hair as if he hadn't a care in the world. "I'm wondering why you're here.

Why did you come back? Surely Janda didn't bring you in her delicate condition."

The fact he knew Janda was pregnant wasn't what bothered me. It was the haughty tone he used. It was a genuine struggle to keep from balling up my fists. Punching him would be playing his game. "Have you been attempting to contact my wife? Her sleep can be fitful, which is understandable at this stage of the pregnancy."

Jasper raised his chin defiantly. "I've only been interested in checking on her well-being. She is a unique woman."

"No arguments there. But hijacking her dreams must mean you want her for something." I prodded him a little more. "What could a pregnant traveler do for you?"

"Nicely done," Jasper said. There was true admiration in his voice. "You've deflected the real issue, which is what do *you* want from *me*?"

"We seem to be at a stalemate," I said. "I want something from you, and you want something from Janda. Why don't we share what we each need and go from there?"

The demon prince took his time thinking about the proposal. He ran his fingers through his long strands of black hair. He closed his eyes then opened them slowly. "Very well. You first."

This was a game where the first person to speak would lose the advantage. He had succeeded in getting the upper hand. It didn't mean I didn't have my own methods of negotiating. I'd been holding back. Now I played my ace.

"It's my understanding that you have a son top-side. It must be hard to keep tabs on him when you're here and he's there. I could arrange to keep you informed of what he's up to. Unless you don't care about what he's been planning." I shrugged.

He was silent.

"Think about it. But don't take too long. Unlike you, I don't have eternity to dwell on decisions."

The ground rumbled beneath my feet. The demon prince worked his jaw back and forth, flaring his nostrils. His eyes darkened. Family relationships could be a touchy subject for many of us, including the prince of the Underworld. I'd touched a nerve.

"I've had many offspring. Only one chose to live in the human world, so I assume we are discussing Stephan. He's a disappointment. He is more human than demon. His nature is weak. As such, he's of little use to me. What he does is no concern of mine. You'll have to do better than that to pique my interest in lending my aid. What do you want, Alexander Holden?"

I'm not the best poker player, but even I could tell his interest in his son was of great concern to him. I had hit the mark or close to it. I now had some leverage to bargain with. At least I hoped that was the case.

"Okay," I said. "Here's the problem. Janda is a beacon to ghosts. They come to seek her assistance with crossing over. Except the Headless Horseman has amassed a large group of them to fight us. He wants revenge for his last encounter with us. He didn't take it well when the mask pieces he sought ended up back in your domain thanks to Janda. She fulfilled her contract with you, which has had repercussions none of us considered. Our weapons have a minimal effect on the onslaught of ghosts. I'm sure you can see my problem."

"What is that to me? Why do you think I have the power to fix what happens in the living realm?"

I gazed around at the decayed landscape with the burned trees and ash-covered boulders. We stood at the edge of an expanse of destruction. "War doesn't happen just in my world. You've seen your share here as well. You've fought the unnaturals, who are a blight to your domain."

He stroked Sasha's head. "You want my weapons?"

"Yes. Without them, the ghosts will continue to attack Janda. I can't let that happen. Can we strike a bargain?"

"Come. I cannot discuss this here."

I'd made my request. What happened next could save my wife and child, so I followed him deeper into the land of decay.

CHAPTER 17

ARMORY

The direction we traveled took us past my hideout. Jasper kept going. I assumed he hadn't discovered my Underworld home. He took me through woods of dead trees and through desolate plains. We finally stopped at a stream. Sasha leaped into the water and began pouncing around. Then she dove deep and didn't surface.

I held my breath, waiting. "Is she okay?"

Jasper walked into the water. "Of course. Now follow my lead." He took three steps forward and dropped out of sight.

"Great. Just great." I mumbled a few choice words under my breath as I moved out into the water, using my foot to test the way. I felt the edge of a drop-off and groaned. I filled my lungs with air, stepped off the ledge, and let myself fall.

As I sank, I kept my eyes open to keep track of my surroundings. The water was dark and murky. I resisted the urge to swim facing down. Jasper had gone feet first, so I did the same. The water temperature grew warmer the farther I went, which was not what I'd expected. Generally, temps plunged going deeper into the water. Not here. I glanced beneath me and saw an orangish glow. Lava? This would not be a good landing.

My feet touched the surface of the glowing embers. While it was hot, it wasn't painful. I felt a tug on my legs. I couldn't swim upward even if I wanted to. I was being sucked into a whirlpool of lava. I closed my eyes and thought of Janda and the baby I'd never lay eyes on because I was about to die.

I didn't die. I didn't even get burned. I fell even farther into the whirlpool.

Thunk.

I hit the base of a lava pit and was immediately tossed upward. I landed in a cave similar to the lava pits where Janda, Hulda, and I had once been in when we exited Jasper's lair. I kneeled for a moment to catch my breath.

"Impressive," Jasper said. "You survived. Not many do."

I raised my head to stare at him. "Lucky me."

He shrugged. "That depends on what you have to offer."

I stood, noting I was completely dry. The Underworld was a damn strange place. Where else would you dive into water, get sucked into a lava whirlpool, and come out the other side without being scorched or soaked to the bone? Thinking was still a slow process. My ears had a slight buzzing going on. I tipped my head to one side and smacked my head as if to dislodge water. My eardrums made a popping sound, and my brain began to catch up with the events. "I suppose what I can offer depends on why you've been trying to connect with Janda."

"Let's stop beating around the bush." Jasper's tone had an edge of annoyance to it. "You want weapons to push back the ghosts and destroy the Headless Horseman. For one thing, you can't destroy the horseman. I made him indestructible. He had certain freedoms with the use of his mask, but now he doesn't have it. He's stuck where he's at and won't be happy until he makes you pay for keeping him tethered to me."

I glared at him. "You're a ray of sunshine. How exactly do we get rid of him?"

"You send him back to Hell."

I deadpanned him. "You're joking. We're just supposed to ship him back to you?"

He shrugged. "Yes. Although, technically, it would be sending him to my father. I'd then be able to bring him here. But you can't do that until you stop Stephan. He's lending power to the horseman, and I can't have that. Stephan may be only half-demon, but he can draw on his demon connection to fuel his limited powers."

There was an interesting dynamic between Stephan and Jasper. My guess was they were in the midst of a power struggle. "He doesn't seem to like you much. It looks like he's thrown his lot in with the horseman to get even with you. That's why you were reaching out to Janda. How is she supposed to stop Stephan or the horseman?"

Sometimes people, even those who were supposed to be intelligent demons, could be incredibly stupid. If we had known how to stop the barrage of spiritual appearances, we would have done it already and I wouldn't be stuck back in the Underworld.

Jasper didn't say a word. But he didn't have to. His rigid expression spoke volumes.

Lava splashed next to me. The aroma of sulfur grew stronger with each stream that flew upward. The space was hot and stuffy. Most of the light came from five lava pits of varying sizes. We were in a cave, but whether it was above ground or beneath the water table of the stream, I wasn't sure. There were two tunnels splitting off in a Y from where we stood. Both were dark. There was no way of knowing if either provided access to an exit. I observed the details of my surroundings while meeting Jasper's gaze. The demon's eyes glowed, showing just how pissed he was with his kid.

"The power that Janda holds is more than either of you could possibly understand. Travelers are rare. It's a gift passed down from mother to daughter." He tilted his head, watching my reaction.

"You're saying my daughter will be like Janda? The baby will be a traveler." It was something the rest of us had tossed around as a possibility, but hearing it from the demon prince was like being doused in icy water.

He sighed. "Just wait until your child begins to test her powers. Parenting a supernatural child with a willful disposition is exhausting. They want more, more, more. It never ends. You ship them off, and still they annoy the shit out of you with their tantrums."

"I see." I had a clear picture of how Jasper had dealt with his half-demon offspring. Ironically, I had been thinking about such things just this week. Being a father scared me. What if I sucked at it?

A smugness came over Jasper's face. "Yes. I can see you do."

"Well, this isn't about my parenting skills. This is about yours. I take it Stephan used to live with you. I'm guessing he was getting on your last nerve, and you cast him out. Now he's causing more trouble just to piss you off." The true problem hit me. I glanced at the demon prince. "He's out of your reach. Janda's the only person you can even hope to connect with to get at your son."

He sneered at me. "Aren't you the smart one? But Janda's pregnancy has made it difficult to contact her. I keep losing the communication thread with her." He grinned. "I didn't have to worry, did I? You came to me. We can help each other."

On the surface, his words made sense. However, I didn't want to find myself tied to him for eternity.

"We can negotiate terms. I require weapons you possess. Once I get them, I can return to my world to take care of the ghosts and get your son to at least talk to you. I still don't know how to send the horseman back to Hell, though."

"Yes. There are some wrinkles in the plan." He stood aside to reveal an opening in the wall behind him. "This is the entrance to my armory."

I stepped closer and peered inside. "There's nothing in there."

"Exactly."

"Are you joking? You don't have weapons? What happened to them?"

"War happened. Most were used to defeat the unnaturals. Afterwards, I was confined to my quarters until your wife enabled my freedom. But my smithy died protecting her. Wart is no longer here to make more weapons that I can infuse with my magic." He stared at me. "I require a new smithy."

I closed my eyes and took a deep breath. This was the hitch I knew would happen. "You're saying I'm your new smithy."

CHAPTER 18

NEW JOB

One of the tunnel openings led to the forge where Jasper's weaponry was made. If I wanted weapons, I'd have to make them myself from the piles of iron and brimstone provided.

"You don't have the fires stoked," I said. "How am I supposed to make any weapons?" My hope of success faltered after I surveyed the space. A huge anvil was stationed near a bucket of water with a hefty-looking hammer on a stone table. There was no flint to strike in order to ignite a fire.

Jasper rolled his eyes. "Your thinking is too concrete. Remember where you are, shifter. Starting a fire is the easy part." He loaded a scoop of coal into the forging pit and blew on it. Flames licked the coals until heat billowed forth and the chunks burned orange and white. "Making the metal malleable and shaping it into swords and knives is the tricky part. It's not a talent I possess. That's why I had Wart. Let's hope for both our sakes you can do half as good a job as he did."

"One sword won't stop the army the Headless

Horseman has gathered. We don't have time for me to make enough to supply my people with weapons."

After scooping another shovel full of coal into the forge pit, Jasper paused to lean on the shovel's handle. "I know what you're up against. That's why it's going to take both of us to make this work. Look at me. I'm reduced to manual labor as a smithy's assistant. I'm a prince of the Underworld. This is *not* what I was born to do. What I *was* born to do is magic. Your job is to make a sword to rival that of the horseman's. My job is to infuse magic into that sword." He stepped back as the fire took hold. He stared into the rising heat vapors. "One sword is all you'll need."

I removed my shirt and set to work, using the bellows to stoke the fire and prod the coals with an iron poker. "Will striking the Headless Horseman down with the sword kill him?"

"It will send him back to me. I'll be ready for him." He picked up a pair of shackles. "He owes penance for his crimes."

"What about Stephan Turner?" Somehow I didn't think felling the demon's son with the sword would go over well with Daddy.

Jasper's eyes glinted reddish-orange. "Cut him down."

My jaw dropped. "You can't be serious. You want me to kill your son?"

"Yes."

This was not what I'd expected. "And if I don't?"

It wasn't just the demon prince's eyes that blazed. His red horns burst into flaming torches that cast a glow against the rock walls. His hair gleamed dark but never caught fire. He waved a hand in my direction, and a burst of pain shot across my chest. I glanced down at the flesh. I'd been tattooed.

"I'm not one of Satan's followers. Get this off of me." I clenched my fists in barely contained rage.

"Stop looking so indignant." He spoke with an air of indifference. "The mark will allow you to ignite the power infused in the sword. Only someone bearing the mark of the leviathan cross can wield the weapon you're about to forge. Before the leviathan cross ever held the connotation of being one of my father's followers, it was something much more simplistic and functional. It's the mark of brimstone."

"Is it permanent?" My chest heaved as I worked to gain control of my emotions.

He shrugged. "I'm not sure. Maybe. Maybe not. I suppose we will find out." He turned to leave, pausing by the entrance. "Oh, you might want to get busy with the sword. I've done all I can. The rest is up to you."

I grit my teeth so hard my jaw ached. I watched the demon prince leave and then threw the forging hammer at the cave wall. "Fuck!"

I'd once took part in a forging class. That was years ago. My success was to be determined by how much I recalled. I found a basic sword mold and laid it out on the forging table. I began the task of scooping the iron that had already been separated from its source. Wart had left a decent supply. I was grateful for his attention to detail and preparedness. Having the smelting already done saved me numerous hours of work.

I used the bellows to thrust air into the forge until the coals grew white with heat. Next, I mixed the extracted iron and brimstone together with no clear idea of the proper proportions of iron to brimstone. I went with my gut and stopped when it had an even consistency between the two materials. In it went to be liquified. Time passed while I waited for the metals to melt so I could pour them into the mold.

I thought of Janda and our baby. Would she ever forgive me if I didn't make it out of the Underworld?

I labored for hours after the initial mold was filled and the sword blank completed. The process of tempering the blade seemed to go on forever. I wiped beads of sweat from my brows and kept at it. Heating, hammering, cooling. After cycle upon cycle of tempering, I started the process of folding so the brimstone and iron fused more strongly. My arms throbbed from the exertion. I couldn't stop. I had to perfect the weapon.

Time in the Underworld was weird. There were no clocks or even a sun to help determine the passing of the hours. None of it mattered here. It mattered in Sleepy Hollow.

Had Janda given birth yet? What about Stephan? If I faced him, would I kill him?

I had no answers, especially for the question of what would happen if I failed.

The sword balanced well in my hands. It was the right size and weight for me. I practiced by doing battle with an imaginary opponent, thrusting and then raising the blade to parry. I pivoted on the balls of my feet, making a sweeping movement with the sword. It was as if it was an extension of my arm. It felt natural to wield it.

Jasper stood in the archway, clapping. His burnt-umber skin glistened in the forge light. "Marvelous. You'll be an assassin among assassins."

I halted. "I'm not your assassin. That's not part of the agreement. My contract is to get both the horseman and your son back to the Underworld."

He strode forward and took the sword from my hands. "You're a natural smithy. I could use someone like you."

I glared at him. "This is a one-time arrangement."

Jasper swung the sword in an arc, parrying and thrusting as I had done. He was graceful. He was a skilled fighter. He was deadly.

"Our agreement is for you to send the horseman back to Hell, where I will put him in shackles for a very, very long time. You're also to kill my son. That makes you an assassin."

"I won't kill Stephan unless he attacks me or mine. If you don't want him back home with you, then I'll hand his ass over to the human authorities."

Laughter bounced off the stone walls. Jasper cleaved a wooden stool in half. I stared at him. Stephan had gotten his batshit-crazy genes from his father.

The act of cutting the stool apart seemed to calm Jasper. He straightened, inhaled for several seconds and then blew the breath out in a puff of smoke. "You *will* kill Stephan. It's the only way for me to grab his ass and haul him home. The moment he draws his last breath, he will be transported back to where he belongs."

The glare from the demon prince sent my way made it clear there was no room for failure. But I had to ask. "What if I can't kill him? What if he escapes?"

"Then you will take his place, so I suggest you fulfill your end of the bargain." He took the sword to the forge, where he stuck it into the hot coals for no more than a minute. When he withdrew it, the metal glowed white with the heat. He took the sword to the anvil, and instead of hitting it with the forging hammer, he blew great breaths of flame onto it. He spoke in an undertone to the sword, flipped it over and blew flames on it again. He repeated this seven times. Then he held it up in front of him with a look of pure pride and joy.

"Catch," he said, sending the sword end-over-end through the air.

I caught it out of pure reflex. The second I made contact, the leviathan cross sent a sharp pain deep into my chest. The sword thrummed with magic. I stared at it and then at Jasper. His lips curled into a smile that sent chills through my bones.

CHAPTER 19
HOMEWARD BOUND

L eaving wasn't as awe-inspiring as the arrival. Jasper took me through the adjoining tunnel. After reaching the end, he shoved a slab door aside and walked out. I followed to find we were back in the land of decay.

"You're shitting me," I said. "We could have just walked through this tunnel to get to the armory?"

"Of course, but where's the fun in that? Besides, I had to know you could survive the lava whirlpool."

"Why?" I was at a complete loss about his damn logic and growing more irate by the second.

"Consider it a rite of passage. You survive, and you get to move on to the next step. Isn't that what life as a shifter is all about? Proving your worthiness to mate with someone as special as Janda?"

I didn't like where he was going with this train of thought. He was attracted to my hot and gifted wife. I couldn't blame him there. I just didn't want him making a claim on her. When I got back, Gwenn would have to work with Janda to teach her to shut and lock the freaking door to the Underworld in her dreams so Jasper couldn't just open it any damn time he wished.

We crossed the barren land and arrived back at the location where I'd first met him. Sasha came bounding up behind him and jumped on my chest. I patted her head and made her get off. She proceeded to sit on my feet and stare eagerly up at me.

"Fine. One more pet before I go." I ran my hand over her head and scratched behind both ears. She got off my feet.

"You're lucky she likes you. Otherwise, it might not be such a good thing to be so close to her. Sasha is what you call a free spirit. She roams where she pleases. She came into my life out of the blue and likely will depart the same way. Sasha's owned by no one."

I had a new appreciation for Sasha. In a way, she reminded me of Janda. Both, it seemed, could cause a heap of chaos. Both were devoted to those they loved. I wondered if Sasha loved Jasper. I had my doubts. He was a passing fancy. Someone to entertain her immortal soul.

Jasper made no attempt to call the dog to his side. "I'll await news about the Headless Horseman and my son. You should know that while the sword isn't like some enchanted carriage that turns back into a pumpkin at midnight, you have a time limit on its magic. You have three days to kill my son. Good luck, Smithy of the Underworld."

He started walking back toward his home but hesitated. He returned to where I stood. "One more thing. The idiot pirate who had Sasha show you the way into the Underworld let loose a few unnaturals into your realm at the same time. When you get back, you might want to dispose of them. And this time, watch what tries to leave with you."

I was going to kill Reggie. I sprinted to where I remembered the entrance was located. Sasha thought it was a great game and raced alongside me. Occasionally, she'd nip at my heels.

"Not now, girl. I have to get home pronto."

The terrain was confusing, but I discovered the tunnel and dove inside. I crawled and shimmied. I shoved the sword in front of me or pulled it behind me inside the tight quarters. When I could, I stood and ran. Sasha barked delightedly behind me. I threw caution to the wind, not caring if unnaturals discovered my presence. Sasha could have them as a snack.

I halted at the spot where the tunnel went straight up and groaned at the sight of jagged rocks protruding from the walls. I glanced at Sasha. "How did you ever get up there?"

She yipped and bounded out of sight. The next thing I knew, she was on a ledge high above me. She sat and stared down at me.

"Okay. Mind showing me how you did that trick?"

The dog seemed to know what I'd asked and backed into an alcove and was gone. She reappeared from behind an outcropping of rocks to my left. She barked, urging me to follow. I gazed around the area, alert to anything trying to hitch a ride out of the Underworld. The space she showed me was tight. I almost couldn't fit. I had to push the sword through the gap and suck in my gut to squeeze through. We climbed a path that ended at the ledge she'd been on before.

I stared up at the dim morning light above us. "Now what?"

Sasha began a hopscotch method of leaping back and forth across the tunnel walls from one ledge to another. I realized she was following a natural path that wound its way to the top. As I drew nearer to the exit, I heard sounds that made my blood chill and my hair stand on end.

I emerged in the middle of a battle between close to a dozen unnaturals and Nick and Damon's shifters. Mutther was nowhere to be seen. He'd vowed to protect Janda. He would be with her. I owed him. Again.

Sasha growled.

She didn't hesitate. She launched herself at the nearest unnatural and dragged it off. Screeches came from where she'd gone. I almost pitied the unnatural she was ripping apart. Another one slashed its bony-clawed hands across Damon's chest and face. Damon howled and fell to the ground. The unnatural had him pinned. I couldn't shift while holding the sword, so I used it. How the magic worked was anyone's guess. I relied on instinct to guide me.

I swung the sword at the creature attacking Damon and lopped off its head. The body slid off Damon, and the head rolled along the ground. There was no inkling that magic had dispatched the unnatural. It seemed like good, old-fashioned cutting it down with the blade at work here, not magic. Sasha returned, saw the head rolling by, and pounced on it. She seemed to think it was a wonderful toy. I kneeled next to Damon. He was a bloody mess.

"Behind you," he cried.

I whipped around to find three more unnaturals coming at me. Holding the sword vertically in front of me, I breathed, searching for the magic of the tattoo. I knew it worked when the sword took on a crimson glow. I charged my attackers, who took one look at the crimson sword and tried to back away. Too late. I swung. One. Two. Three. Each swipe of the sword sliced through one of the unnaturals. The ones who'd been cut fell to the ground and vanished with a loud pop. I almost froze with what actually happened, but caught myself and kept swinging.

Now I understood what Jasper had meant about killing Stephan Turner. Anything from the Underworld that got slashed by this particular sword would be transported back to where they'd come from, as long as I focused on activating the magic.

Nick had shifted and gone after one of the unnaturals. He tore it apart, but like the first one I'd killed with the sword, its body remained on the ground. It didn't disappear. Then Sasha trotted up all happy and bit into the body.

Pop!

It vanished.

Nick shifted back and jogged over to me. "Well, damn, would you look at that?"

"I am looking at it. Or I was until it vanished."

Sasha was in her glory. She chased one after another of the remaining unnaturals, ripping them to pieces and sending them back to the Underworld.

"You should adopt that dog. Damn useful to have around." He backed up when Sasha pranced toward us.

"She won't hurt you."

He didn't look convinced. "Says who?"

"You'd be dead already if she intended you harm." I bent to greet her, and she jumped on me, knocking me to the ground and licking my face. "Enough, Sasha. I don't want a bath."

She hopped off and ran in circles around me before bounding off playfully.

CHAPTER 20

TAINTED BLOOD

The scene where the unnaturals had engaged with the shifters looked perfectly normal—at least from the standpoint of no evidence remaining to indicate the unnaturals had ever been there. Damon was the only injury. He was in rough shape. The bleeding wouldn't stop.

"Why isn't he healing?" Nick said.

I put pressure on the worst cut, but blood kept seeping out. Damon had lost consciousness, which meant he wouldn't be able to shift to heal faster.

"I don't know. Possibly a poison. This is bad. Go get Gwenn and meet us at Sebastian's. The birthing room is pretty well equipped to patch him up. Hopefully, Gwenn knows what's keeping him from healing and fixes it."

"Do you think she can do that?" He leaned over Damon and helped put pressure on the wounds.

"I'm not sure. This isn't normal, even by shifter standards," I said.

Some of Damon's pack members lifted him up and placed him carefully in the back of a truck belonging to one of them. None of the pack besides Damon could get past the wards protecting Sebastian's house, so I hopped in the truck's bed to go with them. The ride was bumpy once we entered the road leading to Sebastian's. I winced each time Damon got jostled.

We pulled over, and I took the wheel to drive the rest of the way.

"I'll send word as soon as I know anything," I said.

The four men who'd escorted Damon got out of the truck and stood numbly by as I drove through the barrier to Sebastian's. I spotted Mutther in his dragon form high above me. His giant wings flattened against his body as he dove closer to the ground to come in for a landing. I met him near the garage. He had already tossed on some clothes and was running to help carry Damon into the house.

"Damn, Alex, this is bad." He picked Damon up and cradled the alpha wolf to his chest as we hurried into the house and to the birthing room.

"Gwenn should be here soon. I sent Nick to the historical society to pick her up." Adrenaline mixed with anxiety fueled my heartbeat to a fast pace. I couldn't let Damon die. It would devastate Janda.

She came rushing out of her new quarters at our approach. "What happened? Is Uncle going to be okay? Crap. That's a lot of blood. Why aren't his wounds healing?"

There was no time to answer her. We laid Damon out on the hospital bed while Janda scurried to bring towels and bandages. She brought a bowl of water and some clean washcloths to wipe away the crusted blood on his face and chest so we could better gauge the extent of his injuries. Aside from a few minor scrapes, there seemed to be just one major cut down the side of his neck that may have nicked his jugular.

"Shit," I said. "He needs stitches."

Janda cleaned more of the scratches. "Sebastian left to get the doctor." Her tone was calm and soothing. She'd gotten past her initial shock and was all about saving her uncle. "What caused the gashes?"

I explained about the unnaturals attacking Damon. I refrained from sharing the details of the sword. That would be a private matter for later.

"Unnaturals? How'd they get out of the Underworld?" She brushed Damon's hair from his forehead, probing for wounds. She glanced up long enough to meet my gaze. "Well?" She would not let it drop.

Mutther gave me a sideways glance. "I'm going to take to the skies. It's time to make a pass through the area. I'll be back in a few."

"Thanks," I said. The undertone of my meaning was clear. *Thanks for ditching me and leaving me in the hands of the inquisitor.*

He didn't bat an eye at abandoning me. "Shout if you need me."

I glared at him. *Nope. He wasn't bailing me out of this one.*

I turned to my loving wife to explain but was spared when Sebastian came in with the doctor.

Dr. Clarence, a shifter from Nick's pack, made quick work of his examination. "What was Damon injured with?"

"Unnaturals from the Underworld. My guess is their claw-like nails are coated in some type of poison that leeched into his bloodstream." I wouldn't meet Janda's gaze. "I have no idea what that poison could be, though. Can you help him?"

Dr. Clarence took a blood sample and began making a

slide to examine under a microscope he'd brought with him. This guy came prepared. "It's hard to say. If I knew what we were fighting, then maybe we'd stand a better chance. Otherwise, I can't make any promises."

Janda blanched. She swallowed hard but never left her uncle's side.

Sebastian strode off to the rear of the house. I heard him greeting Gwenn. She entered the birthing area and went about the process of using her pendulum and crystals to divine the source of the poison by holding them over the wound.

After a few moments, she stepped away from Damon. "I don't know for sure, but I believe we're looking at a very potent venom. Is anyone familiar with what type of spiders or snakes are in the Underworld?"

This was something I knew about. I knew because a monstrosity of a spider had bitten me while I lived in the Underworld. I'd been sicker than I'd ever been in my life. Maude called it a wolf's bane spider. Damn, that was a beastly thing. She'd used a mustard plaster that stung like crazy.

"Have any of you heard of a poisonous wolf's bane spider?" I scanned Sebastian's shelves for anything arachnid related but came up empty.

Janda shook her head no, and so did Dr. Clarence.

Gwenn paled at the suggestion. "Then we better work fast." She pulled out a small dagger from her bag and handed it to me.

"What am I supposed to do with this?" It was a lady's dagger. Small, with a ruby gemstone on the hilt.

"I'll do it," Dr. Clarence said. "But Alex will have to suck out the venom. A mechanical device won't work in this case. The artificial elements of a syringe could interact with the venom and taint the blood worse than before. More importantly, it takes a person's touch to know when the blood is clean."

I stood at the doctor's elbow. "Just tell me what has to be done."

It was Gwenn who answered after giving the doctor a quick glance. "A fresh cut has to be made below the wound. Then the poison drawn out. It's not just dangerous for Damon. You mustn't allow even a drop of the venom to slide down your throat."

"If I do?"

"The best-case scenario is a massive fever and hallucinations while your body burns off the poison." She met my gaze. "You could die, Alex."

"Fabulous," I said. "Note to self. Don't swallow."

"Precisely," Gwenn said. She rummaged in her bag and withdrew a tiny vial of blue liquid. "Here. Drink this. It's a common antidote for most normal spider bites. It may help ease the symptoms if you happen to get any of the poison in your system."

I kissed Janda. "I love you. No matter what happens, you have to know you've been the best thing to happen to me. Ever." I raised the vial to my mouth.

She covered my hand with hers before the vial could touch my lips.

"You better not die, Alex. You have a lot of explaining to do. Don't think dying will get you out of it, either." She kissed me and stepped back for me to chug the antidote.

"Cheers," I said. It was bitter, but I kept drinking. I nodded when I was ready.

Sebastian came in at that point. "What's he doing?"

"Getting ready to suck out the venom," Gwenn said.

"That should be my job. He's more important than I am. He has a family," Sebastian said.

"I'm sorry," Gwenn said. "Not to be mean, but Alex's time in the Underworld makes him the best one for the job."

Sebastian looked grim. "Very well. But know that I will always protect your family, Alex."

"I know. Thank you."

Gwenn cast a spell of purity over the dagger. The ruby brightened and then dimmed. She handed it to Dr. Clarence. He bent close to Damon and made a careful incision a couple of inches below the wound. Blood trickled out. He put pressure on the incision.

"All yours," he said, glancing up at me.

I traded places with him and lowered my mouth to the wound. Damon's blood had a stench of death that reminded me of the decayed lands in the Underworld. I began drawing out the poison one mouthful at a time and spitting it in a bowl. I prayed this would work and I'd cheat death one more time.

CHAPTER 21

THEORIES AND REVELATIONS

The birthing center stunk of decay, but Damon was resting easy and I hadn't keeled over yet. I'd take that win. Damon's pack celebrated with whoops and runs through the surrounding woods in their wolf forms. We were still on alert and careful to maintain high levels of security throughout Sleepy Hollow, but the packs deserved to let off some steam.

Sebastian called for a meeting to go over our options. Silas was the only one not coming. He remained vigilant in the area around the tunnel to the Underworld, watching for any further breaches until we could close that entry point to our world. Sasha had curled up on the boulder and gone to sleep. We took that to be a good thing. Between Silas, his shifters, and Sasha, that part of our paranormal problem was covered. It was the ghost population that worried me. We had yet to contain it.

Normally, we'd meet in Sebastian's study to hash out a strategy, but not this time. With Damon recovering, we opted to meet in Janda's new quarters. None of us minded moving the location, since this was the most technologically advanced spot in the entire house. The solar panels provided enough electricity to charge our phones and have decent lighting. But cramming all of us into the space was a challenge. I'd sent a text to Sid to join us, and Shawn was coming to update us on the surveillance of Stephan Turner.

Gwenn insisted on removing the negative energy in the birthing room. She shooed us all into the hall so she could do a smudging of the room to cleanse the space before the baby was born. Damon was allowed to stay, but I could tell he'd rather be with the rest of us in the hall than with Gwenn.

The smudging with sage and other herbs didn't take long. When it was over, Gwenn added several vases of fresh-cut flowers to brighten the room and bring in natural beauty she said was essential for the baby. It was also a much better smell than the stench of the poison I'd extracted from Damon. After getting a whiff of the unnatural's venom, I was certain I'd found the origin of our invasive stink bug population. Here was proof those things were a byproduct of the Underworld and sent to torment us.

Janda sank into a cushy upholstered chair that had been set next to Damon's bed. Hudson had been wandering through the house and followed us into the room, where he claimed his spot on Janda's lap.

She stroked his fur. "I get the stuff about Jasper, or at least what he shared with Alex, but what's with the dog?"

"I can elaborate once the others get here," I said.

She pursed her lips. "Fine. Don't tell me."

"It's not like that, love."

Her emotions were erratic at the moment. I chalked it up to her raging hormones, but Gwenn seemed to believe Janda's magic was being affected by the pregnancy and causing fluctuations in Janda's moods. This was yet another reason I couldn't wait until the baby was born.

We did our best to get comfortable while we waited for Shawn, Angie, and Sid. It was standing room only. No one cared. We were happy to count Damon among our ranks of the living and would accommodate him however possible.

"Stop fussing over me," he said. "I'm not dying."

"Thanks to Alex," Janda said, putting her hand in his.

He groused about the added attention, but I think he secretly enjoyed it. He kept a tight hold on Janda. I caught him periodically sneaking a glance her way when she wasn't looking. They may have had a rocky start during her childhood, but not now. They had a solid bond. I took that nugget of insight and tucked it away for when my daughter began stirring up trouble. The anticipation of a mini-Janda in my life made me smile. I was truly blessed.

Feet tapped. Arms crossed and uncrossed. An undercurrent of impatience spread through the room. I had to do something. "I think we can begin without the others. We can fill them in on the bigger picture later."

"Finally," Janda said. "I've been on pins and needles for ages anticipating you sharing your escapades."

There was more than a little snark in her tone. Yeah, she was still pissed that I'd gone to the Underworld and had withheld information.

I poured a cup of herbal tea and handed it to her. "Love, it's been less than an hour."

She took a sip of her tea. "Seemed like longer to me, but fine. Whatever. Get on with it."

I shook my head at her impatience. "Drama much?"

"No. Not really," she said. "Not when I'm the one shut away while everyone else comes and goes as they please. No drama here." Her agitation about being excluded from anything that would get her away from Sebastian's was abundantly clear.

I made a mental note to get her outside tonight. It would do us both good to have some alone time. I gazed around the room at everyone who'd come and was grateful for this family of close friends I'd found. I waited for them to settle down before starting. My phone buzzed. I read the text Sid sent. He was waiting to be escorted through the barrier.

"Sebastian, would you mind getting Sid past the protection spells? He's waiting at the boundary line."

"Of course. I'll only be a moment." He took off in a flash that made his image blur.

"I guess he doesn't want to miss anything," Nick said.

We all laughed. It was good to break the tension and joke a little.

Sebastian returned shortly with Sid, Shawn, and Angie. He practically shoved them into the tight quarters. "Now you may begin your tale."

I suppressed a grin and started the narrative with my meeting with Sid. Most of the people here already knew this part of the saga, but not Janda.

"Jasper has a grown kid? Here?" Janda's brows nearly reached her hairline.

Hudson hissed before going back to napping on Janda's lap.

"That explains a lot," Gwenn said. She strode off to get her smudging tools. "We are going to have a great deal of cleansing to do." She sat on a chair next to Janda, armed with her witchy implements as if she'd need them at any moment.

I continued but kept getting interrupted every minute or two with questions. They wanted to know how the prince of the Underworld reacted when I mentioned Stephan Turner to him. They wondered what Stephan had done to get kicked out of his daddy's house. Where was Mommy Dearest? I answered what I could, and we speculated about the rest. I could tell Janda was getting tired and wanted to move things along. We all agreed that the unnaturals escaping to our realm had to be fixed. The portal would have to be destroyed.

"Sasha can kill unnaturals?" Janda said. "I have to meet this dog."

Damon spoke in a rough whisper. "Why did the sword not kill the unnaturals? Or did it? I'm confused."

I tried to explain as best as I could. "I believe Sasha can kill them instantly. She likes to play with them first. But the sword can only kind of kill them. They die on this plane but can only return to the Underworld if I fully activate the sword. Then Jasper gets his chance to make them suffer."

Sebastian sipped a glass of red wine that he'd gone and poured for himself and returned without me even noticing. We started tossing around theories and concluded that Jasper had infused the sword with a certain amount of magic, which he fashioned to his specific requirements. He didn't want me to kill his son, at least not permanently.

"So Alex has to find Stephan and use the sword to send him back to Jasper. Stephan doesn't really die. But Sasha doesn't have limits on her magic and can destroy supernatural threats completely. Is that right?" Janda said.

"It would appear so," I said.

"You know," Gwenn said. "That makes perfect sense. Jasper withholds his full magic so you're forced to comply with his wishes. You also wouldn't be able to use the sword against him. That's darn good. I wish I could do selective magic."

Mutther had been leaning against the wall and now moved to sit on the arm of Gwenn's chair. "If all this is true, then we have to take out Stephan Turner as soon as possible. Send his ass home to Daddy, and the horseman loses access to the power that has enabled him to haunt our lives for so long."

It was Shawn's turn to share what he'd seen. "The guy is a creep. But my men have seen nothing unusual. The guy bar hops in the middle of the day. He's so sloshed by nighttime that his mouth spouts off all sorts of idiotic bullshit. I believe he may be acting."

"He's acting the part of a drunk?" Nick said. "Why?"

Shawn pulled out his small notebook and began reciting dates, times, places, and activities. "There's a trend. Each time Turner goes into a bar, his site gets tons of hits. I think he's recruiting."

"There are many kinds of stupid in this world. Sounds like he's found his niche," Sebastian said. "Keep on him. He'll slip up. His kind always do."

"But what about the ghosts? Who do they really follow?" Janda's brows knitted when she was worried. Her brows were knitted now.

"That's a great question," I said. "The only sure way to find out is to draw Stephan Turner into the open and force his hand. If the ghosts follow his orders, and not the horseman's, that will be our answer."

"I like it," Nick said. "Action instead of overthinking it."

I sighed. "That's not what I meant."

He shrugged. "That's what you said."

I shook my head and gave up.

"I have a question," Janda said. "There's also the stuff Sid mentioned with the tech device functioning with a magical power cell. Does that mean Stephan Turner is dealing in shady magical tech?" She glanced at Sid, who stood next to a cabinet filled with antique medical oddities that had caught his attention. "Do I have that right, Sid?"

He half-turned to answer, keeping one eye on the cabinet. "Oh. Yes. I'd say that is an accurate description of how these tech devices run. In fact, the power cell is an excellent descriptor." He returned to surveying the objects in the case. "What *is* this thing?" He picked up the dried-up body of slug and held it aloft.

Sebastian took it and placed it back in the cabinet. "It's a mummified leech." He glanced at Sid. "Don't touch. You never know what might come back to life. One drop of your blood, and that baby leech will latch on and suck you dry."

Sid blinked several times. He glanced at the leech. "A *baby* leech? How big does it get?"

Sebastian locked the cabinet door. "You don't want to know."

Nick strode over for a closer look. "Are you telling me the leech corpse thingy can come back to life? That's insane."

"That's vampirism," Sebastian said.

I glanced at Janda. Her pupils were as big as black marbles. Yeah. The shit in that cabinet was going. I didn't want to imagine what the hell Sebastian thought we'd use that stuff for. None of it was going near my wife or baby.

CHAPTER 22

SLEUTHING

The hours passed. We all had the same information now but couldn't agree on what to do with it. Sebastian was off to relieve Silas and update him on the little we'd come up with. Much to Nick's displeasure, we decided not to interfere with Stephan Turner quite yet. Sid wanted the actual tracking device and went with Shawn to sign it out of the evidence locker at the station house. Gwenn had some research to conduct, so Mutther said he'd escort her to the historical society. From the glances they kept giving each other, I was sure their *research* would have more of a physical approach than a scholarly one. I coughed to hide my grin.

"You can't go, too, Uncle," Janda said. "I won't have anyone to talk to."

Damon had dressed and was shuffling toward the door. "Sorry, Niece, this is not where I belong."

I walked him to the back door and gave him the keys to a black Mercedes that Sebastian said he could borrow. Several pack members would be waiting on the other side of the barrier.

"I owe you," he said. His movements were slow and pained as he got into the car.

"You owe me nothing." I was concerned about him driving in such a weakened state. "Just don't wreck Sebastian's car."

He snorted. "That old vampire can eat my shorts."

"Your funeral," I said.

He snorted again and started the engine. He drove off, weaving from one side of the driveway to the other.

"Shit. He's going to wreck it." I groaned at the thought of telling Sebastian his car was a piece of scrap metal.

Janda came up behind me. "Nah. He's just messing with you."

Sure enough. Damon revved the engine and tore off through the barrier.

"Asshole," I said.

Janda laughed. "Never mind him. I'm hungry."

I realized I had eaten nothing during my stay in the Underworld. There was little to eat there on an average day, let alone on a day where I was sweating at a demon's forge. The everything bagel from earlier wasn't enough. I was famished. One look at Janda, and I knew I had to risk taking her into town. It wasn't exactly the outing I wanted to do for her, but it would have to suffice. I sent a message to Mutther so he'd know where Janda would be and to do a sweep through the area we would travel through.

I tapped out a text to Gwenn. *I'm taking Janda to the bagel shop.*

My phone pinged. *Perfect! I'll meet you there in thirty minutes. Still researching.*

I'd give them extra time in case the *researching* required more than thirty minutes. I knew from my experience with Janda that we often had to check our *research* twice. The memories of those intimate moments had my cock stiffening. I pushed those thoughts aside and followed Janda inside.

"Sebastian's kitchen is dismal as ever, but I have a stash of food in my room."

She started for the new quarters, but I grabbed her hand. I pulled her into a kiss and released her before my cock got the wrong idea. "Tonight is your night. We're going to town for dinner."

Her eyes lit up. "Really? Oh, that would be so amazing. You have no idea how much I could use a night out."

"Don't get too excited. We're only going to the bagel shop. I promise once this crap with the horseman and Turner is over that I'll take you for a steak dinner."

She put a hand on my cheek. "You idiot. I don't need steak dinners. All I want is you. And also a fresh bagel. And also to go pee right now." She laughed and waddled off to her new private bathroom.

The sword was where I'd left it in an umbrella stand outside Janda's door. Gwenn insisted it remain out of the birthing room so as not to contaminate the space with what she called "unclean energy." I didn't mind leaving it there when I was in the house, but outside was different. It had already proven useful. I opened the tiny cabinet where Sebastian kept his keys. Riding Miss Kitty or my Harley was not happening.

Janda met me outside. She looked from Miss Kitty to the Mercedes SUV I'd parked next to the rear entrance. She frowned. "Okay, fine. I can't risk anything happening to the baby. I don't think I could straddle Miss Kitty anyway. Besides, driving her with the sword in tow is an issue."

"Sorry," I said. "Think of it as practice for when the baby

arrives. We won't be having a car seat on the back of our motorcycles."

"True." She made a circle around the SUV before taking a peek inside. "This is pretty nice. Plenty of room in the back for the baby. We should shop for one of these." She went over to her bike and patted the leather seat. "You'll always be my girl. This doesn't mean we won't have good times together. It's just that our family is getting bigger. You understand, right?"

I raised my brows at her. "It's a motorcycle, love, not a person."

She glared at me. "That's what you think. Miss Kitty has saved my bacon more times than I can count. She's not *just* a motorcycle." She huffed and got into the SUV.

"Okay. I stand corrected." Arguing would get us nowhere, and we'd be late. I got in and drove us through the barrier. This wasn't a good start to the evening.

We rode along the winding road toward town at a good pace. Dusk was settling in and so was the unease in my gut. Doubts about leaving the safety of Sebastian's had me checking the rearview mirror every few seconds.

"We'll be fine," Janda said. "You have your magic sword, and Mutther has been flying overhead for the past few minutes. Relax."

She was right, but I couldn't relax. I parked in front of the bagel shop door but wouldn't let her out until I did a quick scan of our surroundings.

"Clear," I said. "Let's get you inside."

The shop was closed, but all it took was one call from Gwenn for George to agree to let us have the place to ourselves. I was afraid it would be a hard sell after the baby shower fiasco, but George didn't hold that against us.

Gwenn greeted us and hauled us both to a table in the

back corner. George came out of the kitchen carrying a tray of assorted bagels and pastries. Janda's eyes lit up at the goodies.

"Aww, George. That's fantastic. Thanks," Janda said. Her stomach rumbled as George got closer, and the sugary scents washed over us.

"For my favorite momma-to-be. Enjoy." He placed the tray at the center of the table and scurried off to bring the coffee.

Gwenn handed us each a plate and put a fourth one next to her. I assumed it would be for Mutther. George returned with the coffee, and after pouring us each a cup, he sat down to join us. He picked out a cheese danish and put it on his plate. I liked George but didn't know why he was there and not Mutther.

Gwenn couldn't sit still. She had trouble containing her excitement. "So, I did some digging, and with George's help, I think we know who Stephan Turner's mother is."

I dropped my bagel on my plate. "Are you sure? Shawn and Sid haven't been able to track her down and they have access to databases you don't."

She grinned and put her arm around George's shoulder. "They didn't have George for sourcing information."

It was George's turn to smile. "This is true."

Janda swallowed a bite of her bagel. "What did you find out?" She took another bite, never taking her gaze off George.

He puffed his chest out. "Gwenn showed me a picture of that mysterious device, and I recognized the design."

If it was possible for the air not to stir, then that would be what it was like inside the bagel shop. He had our full attention.

"I know a person who knows a person, if you get my

drift, and that other person brought me a brooch once upon a time. The brooch was exquisite. It had a yellowish stone in the center. The person called it brimstone. Now I'd never seen a stone like it, so I couldn't say for sure if it was brimstone. He and his woman companion claimed it was a family heirloom. He said the devil himself couldn't make a nicer piece. That's what the fellow said. His words. Not mine." George took a breath and kept on talking. "It was a gift from his father to his mother. The parents split. He lived with his father but hated being there and ran off to find his mother."

George sat back and drank some coffee. He didn't say anything else.

I stared at him. "Is that it?"

"What do you mean, is that it? Of course it isn't. A guy has to wet his whistle once in a while when he's telling a tale." He drank more coffee.

I took a breath and let it out slowly. "Are you good to go now?"

He took another sip. "Sure." He glanced at everyone and continued. "So, this guy was thinking of finding a buyer for this brooch he had. He said it was to fund a tech project. My job was to find a buyer, which I did. The transaction went fine. Everyone was happy."

"Until they weren't?" I said.

George nodded. "You got it. The buyer ended up dead, and the brooch—"

"Was gone," I said.

"No way," Gwenn said. She'd been on the edge of her seat during the entire story.

Janda narrowed her eyes at George. "Was the buyer a woman, by any chance?"

It was George's turn to sit there with his mouth open. "Yeah. It was. How'd you know that?"

She leaned forward as much as her belly would allow. "I watch crime shows. I know stuff."

I glanced at my wife. "Since when do you watch crime dramas?"

She gave me a smug look. "Since Sebastian got me a TV."

"You're streaming shows now?" I was stuck on the concept of my shifter wife watching crime shows.

"You try being pregnant and isolated."

Gwenn reached across for Janda's hand. "Alex doesn't understand these things. There's no judgement here. Please. Tell us what you think happened. George was under the impression the jewelry belonged to the man's mother, and they had to sell it." She glanced at George. "Didn't you say his lady companion was the mother?"

"Now that you mention it, he never introduced her. I assumed the woman was his mother. She was older. A pretty brunette. On the quiet side. He did the talking. The man was Stephan Turner. Gwenn showed me a picture, and I'm positive it was him."

Janda shook her head. "The guy might have been Turner, but the woman wasn't his mother. It's lucky for you I watch this stuff. The woman was a decoy. A distraction. She's unimportant. He could have picked her up off the street to play the part. Anyway, the woman who bought the brooch was the mother who owned the damn thing in the first place. Our friend Turner must have stolen it. He killed his own mother and took the brooch back. He got money from her and got the brooch. She probably refused to fund his tech project, so he got mad."

I was stunned. Absolutely stunned. My wife had become an amateur detective. And I'd bet anything she was right.

CHAPTER 23

ARRIVAL

Before I'd let Janda leave the bagel shop, I shifted and did a perimeter check. One or two ghosts floated around aimlessly but wandered out of town before I had to return to the shop and shift back to use the sword on them. This made me aware of yet another issue with the sword. I couldn't carry it when I shifted, so it limited how far away I could be if I had to get to it fast.

It used to be we couldn't see the apparitions unless they joined up with the horseman. That no longer was the case. Gwenn said it had to do with the number of spirits congregating in one area. Their combined energy made them visible to the human eye more often than not. That made Angie's job a lot harder. She started telling the public that some committee members who organized the October activities were testing holograms of ghosts. So far, residents of Sleepy Hollow accepted that excuse. Angie earned her salary and then some.

We were halfway to Sebastian's house when Janda caught her breath and held her abdomen. "Oh." She let out a breath. "My water broke."

I pulled over to the side of the road. "What do you need me to do?" I was a wreck.

She sucked in another breath and exhaled. "Contractions. I think we're good until we get back to Sebastian's."

I texted Gwenn and Sebastian, fumbled with the phone, and dropped it on the floorboard.

"Oh!" Janda gripped the door handle. "Maybe we should hurry."

Adrenaline shot through me as well as a heavy dose of panic. I swung back onto the road and floored it. "I'm so sorry, love. This is my fault. I should never have taken you into town."

She puffed out a few quick breaths. "Shut up and drive."

"Dammit." I swerved into the other lane to avoid a group of ghosts that appeared in front of the car. I didn't slow. I sped down the road as fast as the car and the curves allowed. "Hold on, love."

She didn't answer. She was too busy using the labor breathing techniques. "This is big. Ahhhh!"

"I'm hurrying." I swerved again to avoid a pothole.

Janda grabbed my arm. "Stop. Have to stop."

We still had several miles to go before reaching Sebastian's. Stopping by the side of the road near Sleepy Hollow was not a good idea. "Are you sure? Can you hold it?"

She hit me. "What the hell are you saying? Hold it? Tell that to your kid, who wants out NOW!"

"Oh, Christ! Okay." I skidded to a stop on a side road that I knew led to the ruins of Hulda's hut. This may be a good omen ending up here. I prayed it was. Regardless, I didn't have time to worry about it.

Janda let out a loud wail. "Ohhhhh!" She reached a new octave on the last note.

I jumped out of the SUV and put the rear seats down

flat. Janda opened her door and scooted out, hanging on to the doorframe for support as she worked through another contraction.

"This is not how I wanted to have our baby," she said. Her words came out in a breathless torrent with curses tossed in for good measure.

I was starting to have a panic attack. My brain refused to function. I couldn't think straight. My wife was having our baby on the side of the road! I tried to get her into the back, but she wouldn't budge.

"Nope. Not moving," she said.

All those baby books I read to prepare us for this momentous event never mentioned the reality of bringing a new life into this world. No, they did not. Nowhere did they remotely describe the utter horror of seeing the mother of your child in so much agony and the helplessness to do anything about it. Where was the freaking book about giving birth on the side of the road with nothing but the shirt on your back? If I survived this night, I'd write that book.

As shifters, we didn't have many inhibitions about our bodies. That was a good thing because Janda started taking off her pants. I bent to help her, and she pushed me away. Okay. Women had been giving birth with little to no help for centuries. The best thing for me to do was to give her space.

One pant leg got stuck on her foot. She kicked her leg out and screeched at the contraction ripping through her. "Well, are you going to help get these damn pants off me or not?"

Okay, then. Don't give her space.

I waited for her to stop kicking her leg. She didn't stop. She kept trying to shake the pants off. I dove in and snatched the fabric in one hand and tugged. It came loose so fast that I lost my balance and landed on my ass. At least they were off. But then Janda tugged at her maternity underwear. I didn't realize she'd started wearing them. She usually went all-natural because of shifting. She'd even given up wearing socks. Less trouble when shifting on-the-fly. She let go of the underwear and pulled at her shirt.

The shirt was easy. I ripped the front apart. It hung open to allow for better movement. Now I had to figure out how to get her underwear off without suffering a grave injury. It was like taking underwear off a bucking bronco. She was flailing every which way. I did the only thing a guy could do. I tore that sucker off her. She nodded and tried to grin. Then another contraction drove into her and a tear fell down her cheek. *Dammit.* My wife was not the crying sort. This was bad.

A downburst of air hit us, grabbing our attention.

Flap. Flap. Flap.

Dragon wings snapped up and down as Mutther settled to the ground. He crouched low. Gwenn had been holding onto his neck. She slid off and darted forward, holding a large duffle bag.

She bent over Janda's hunched form. "It's okay. I'm here. We've got this covered. Just like we planned." Gwenn glanced at me. "How far apart are the contractions?"

"Gwenn. I love you, but shifters rarely wear watches. How am I supposed to know how far apart they are?" I hadn't even thought to time them. I was going out of my mind. Timing contractions absolutely wasn't happening.

She glanced at her watch. "Okay. Janda, we need to get you into the car so I can set things up. Can you help us do that?"

Janda nodded through gritted teeth as a contraction gripped her.

Gwenn glanced at her watch. "Switch places with me, Alex. I'll lay out a blanket, and then if you could carry Janda to the back, that would be great."

I was slow to process her words. She grabbed my arm and shook it.

"Alex? Listen to my voice. Don't worry. We can get through this. You have to switch places with me." She spoke slowly and calmly. She timed the contractions. "Two minutes apart."

We swapped spots, and Gwenn hurried to get the blanket laid out and create a workable space for Janda to give birth. I glanced at Mutther. He stayed in his dragon form, and after surveying the surroundings, he lifted into the air and made ever-widening circles above us.

I carried my wife to the back of the car and placed her gently on the blanket. I moved out of the way to allow Gwenn space to set up her birthing supplies. She had everything from towels to a suction bulb. After a quick examination, she pulled me off to one side.

"As far as I can tell, the baby is in the proper position, so that's good," she said.

Some of the tension left me just knowing the baby was doing fine. "What do I do now?"

"You take this cloth and wipe her forehead while she works through the contractions. They're getting closer together. This is a fast labor. Maybe too fast. I don't know. But she'll need you by her side. Can you do that?"

I nodded. The labor could have complications. I put those fears aside and focused on my wife.

Sebastian came at us in a blur of motion, halting at the rear of the car. "Is she okay? Should we fetch the doctor?"

Gwenn glanced at Janda and then at us. "It's too late. We have to do the delivery here." She took latex gloves from her bag, cleaned her hands with alcohol, and put on the gloves. She spoke over her shoulder while tending to Janda. "She's around 9 cm dilated. Get ready. The baby will be here soon."

I took my position near Janda's head, wiping the beads of sweat forming on her forehead. "Did you hear Gwenn? Our Wrenley will arrive soon. I'm so proud of you, love."

I glanced at my wife and gasped. The glow emanating from her was divine. She illuminated the entire back of the car. Then I caught my breath for a different reason. Ghosts would sense her.

The cloth was dripping with her sweat. I put it down. "I'm getting a new cloth, love. I'll be right back." I stepped out of the car and motioned for Sebastian.

"She's glowing," he said.

"No shit." I lowered my voice so only Sebastian could hear. "She'll have every ghost for miles around alerted to her presence. Call in our security forces to cordon off the area while she's giving birth."

"Understood," Sebastian said. He took off into the darkness in yet another blur of motion.

I glanced skyward. Mutther continued circling. I found my phone in the car and sent out texts to alert everyone of what could soon become a war zone and not a birthing area. Several pings came in at once. Damon was sending a unit pronto. Nick and Shawn would have their people here in fifteen minutes. Silas was on his way with my clan. I pulled the sword from the car and kept it by my side, which was pretty awkward when I crawled back inside to get to Janda.

She glanced at the sword and nodded. She understood and accepted that we could have unwanted visitors.

"She's crowning," Gwenn said. Her voice was filled with excitement that spilled over to the rest of us. She began reciting a spell that spoke of ease and love.

I kissed Janda's forehead. "You've got this."

She squeezed her eyes shut and breathed through a contraction then sucked in a sharp breath. Her eyes widened, but she held it together and focused on Gwenn's singsong chant.

The night held its breath with her, and the trees swayed quietly in the breeze of Mutther's flight path. The moon was a circle of yellow-orange, periodically hidden by passing clouds. A few owls hooted to one another. A message perhaps. Even the creatures of Sleepy Hollow took notice of the new arrival.

The pushing started after the last contraction. No more breathing through it. Janda gripped my hand on the next spasm and pushed. She was tiring. I wiped her forehead as another spasm tore through her. She inhaled and pushed again as Gwenn took hold of the baby's head to guide her out of the birth canal.

The head and then one shoulder popped out. Gwenn eased the other shoulder through the opening. Within seconds our daughter emerged and started crying.

Gwenn worked fast, suctioning the baby's mouth and nose to help with breathing. She clamped the umbilical cord and wiped her off before placing our daughter on Janda's bare chest.

"You did it, love. Wrenley is beautiful." I smiled so much that my cheeks ached. I couldn't help it. My wife and baby were fine. "Lord, she has a full head of hair." I brushed the fine black strands back and caught my breath. "Janda. Look. She has the same white streak that you have!"

"Wow," she said, gazing lovingly at our daughter. "How is that possible?"

"It doesn't matter how. She's amazing." I kissed Janda, sensing a deeper connection with her. The birth of our daughter solidified our mate bond.

Gwenn swaddled the baby and put her back on Janda. "She looks just like you, Janda. And the white streak is so darn cute! Congratulations! This is so thrilling. "

I met Gwenn's gaze. "Thank you. I owe you."

"Being part of the birth is all the thanks I need. Wrenley is exquisite."

She cleaned up and packed everything away while we cooed to our daughter. Wrenley opened her eyes and stared up at Janda.

I kissed the top of Wrenley's head. "Hello, my beautiful little girl. Mommy and Daddy love you."

I was so immersed in the miracle of our daughter's birth that I had dropped my guard. Chaos erupted outside the SUV, breaking in on our moment as a family. I glanced out the window to see a line of ghosts across the width of the road. I picked up the sword and went to face my enemies.

CHAPTER 24

DEFENDER

Mutther launched a stream of fire at the ghosts. A few fell back, most continued forward. These were the malicious kind. Other spirits, timid and hesitant, stayed away from the battle. I didn't want them getting close, either. Janda was too exhausted to face needy apparitions. They hovered in place, watching.

More ghosts filled the road behind the first line. They pushed forward. Their combined energy had a force that hit me and sent me backward.

I dug in my heels and raised the sword. "Stay back!"

They paused, but not because of me. They opened their ranks to let a man join them at the front. He wore a dark jacket that came down to his knees. I knew him even though I hadn't met him before. He had the black hair of his father. His face was also angular with sharp features but his skin held no hint of the umber coloring of his father's complexion. His eyes blazed with the glint of demon orange. There was no mistaking Stephan Turner for anything but the demon that was his genetic nature.

He grinned at me. "I've heard about you, Alexander

Holden. I've even analyzed your security tech from your firm. Not too shabby. But not as good as mine."

He held up an insect-like drone the size of his palm. Embedded in the center of its back wings glowed tiny golden crystals that had to be brimstone. He let it loose, and it flew upward toward Mutther. On its vertical trajectory, the wings sprouted spikes like a porcupine. A few of the spiked quills shot toward Mutther, who had to spiral away from the attack. Stephan ignored his creation's progress. His gaze was on me. It was a challenge. He was an egomaniac bent on proving himself to be the best. I realized too late that Stephan Turner wasn't trying to get to Janda and the baby so much as he was trying to get to *me*. Controlling the Underworld portal by using Wrenley's power, like he'd let the ghosts believe, was nothing compared to destroying me and everything I cared about.

I was his target.

He wanted to prove his superiority to Daddy and the world.

I used his narcissism to poke at his defenses. I held the sword out to my side. "You're not the only one with magic-infused devices. Your demon prince father helped me make this." I swung it in a figure eight. "This is equal to, if not better than, anything you created. Don't you agree?"

Stephan seethed. His eyes glowed reddish-orange. Yeah. There was Daddy's boy.

"You are nothing," he said. "Your sword can't protect you from my magical devices." He produced a second of the drone insects. He whispered to it and set it free. This drone was like an ultra-large mosquito with one hell of a lethal tip to stab its enemies.

The mosquito drone flew directly at my head. I waited until it was near and sliced it in half with the sword. The blade hummed. The gem in the hilt glowed. Two could play at this game. The drone kept coming, but this time it had two sections charging at me. I swung the sword again but put more intention into the desired outcome. The insect dropped to the earth and flickered before its light died out.

Stephan clapped his hands. "Bravo."

"Thanks," I said. "How about you call it a day and take a vacation to see your dad? I know he would love to spend time with you."

The baffled expression on Stephan Turner's face lasted but a moment before he recovered. "You jest. My father couldn't care less where I am or what I do. He gave up his fatherly rights ages ago."

I placed the sword tip-down in front of me and crossed my hands over its hilt. "That's where you're wrong. He does care."

Stephan laughed. "You're so gullible. All my father cares about is himself. Going home would mean living under his roof and his conditions. So, no, thanks."

While Stephan bashed his father, Mutther was still dodging the drone. He banked hard to the left and swung back around to smack the crap out of it with his wing. The drone went rocketing to the ground and smashed. Stephan glanced in that direction before returning his attention to me.

"I suppose 'family' is a bad word for you," I said. "I mean, who kills their own mother? And for what? A chunk of stone and a bit of cash."

I tapped my fingers on the sword hilt and listened for the sound of my daughter. I prayed Janda could let the babe suckle to keep her quiet. There was no way Stephan, his drones, or the ghosts would touch my family. That was the difference between Stephan Turner and me. The guy would never understand family love and would never hold the esteem of those around him.

"My mother was a selfish human who had the bad fortune to travel to the Underworld and fall in love with a demon prince who promised her the world and ditched her. She was far better off dead."

It was sad to see that Stephan believed what he said. I felt sorry for him. He was a lost soul. He mentioned his mother traveling to the Underworld, which meant she was like Janda and able to cross the veil of death. I also understood humans couldn't last in the Underworld when they were supposed to be in the living realm. If I hadn't gotten out, I'd have gone mad. I would have become an unnatural.

"It must suck to be you," I said. I kept him talking to buy time for Nick and the others to get here. As long as Stephan talked, his ghosts stayed put.

"Hardly," he said. "Look what I've amassed and how famous I am for my work. My life will only get better once you are no longer in my sphere with your safe-room technology."

"If you're so powerful and hold such prestige, then why join forces with the horseman? He can't offer you what you seek." I'd been keeping an eye out for the Headless Horseman, who had not come with Stephan. I wondered why.

Stephan was getting agitated and kept glancing behind him. My gut was telling me he'd expected the horseman to be here by now. He needed him as his defender. It was as if we were going to duel, but he had his second stand in for him. Stephan knew he couldn't defeat me. He was putting his faith in the horseman, and that would be his undoing. It seemed Prince Jasper was correct. His son was weak. But it didn't mean he wasn't dangerous.

The downside to keeping Stephan busy was the

growing number of ghosts joining his league of apparitions. They kept coming. At first, they came one or two at a time, but then they came in groups. I got it now. The strategy of the horseman was to gather his forces and send them here. I suspected he would make his appearance soon. I couldn't help but compare our situation with Hulda's during the Revolutionary War where two sides repositioned their forces to gain the upper hand. The winner of this confrontation was yet to be decided.

Mutther continued to patrol the skies. He would wait for a signal from me before launching another offensive maneuver. My panther wanted out. I felt the restlessness within and the urge to spur into action. I scanned the ghost ranks. There were hundreds of them. One sword could not take them all out before some would get past me and reach the SUV and the precious lives it held. I gauged my chances of taking Stephan out before the ghosts could stop me from killing him. The odds weren't in my favor. Still, I considered it.

The ground rumbled beneath me with the tremor of feet racing this way. It made my heart soar. The balance of forces was changing. As soon as my fellow shifters got closer, I'd make my move. I gripped the sword and lifted it an inch or two off the ground. My gaze centered on Stephan. Soon. Just a few more minutes.

He seemed to sense the difference and took a step forward. Stephan Turner wanted me dead. He wanted it bad.

"This is your chance, Turner. Fight me one-on-one. Winner gets the tech world for their own. What do you say?"

I didn't mention that I didn't own squat in the tech world. There were powerful circles that didn't include me.

For some reason, he connected me with his pathway to success. I stood in his way. He was too blind to see he stood in his own way.

He pulled another of his tech drones from his jacket pocket. It unfurled and expanded to become a metallic bronze falcon that sat upon his shoulder and let out a screech that sent shivers down my backside. The falcon's eyes were made of brimstone and the beak of obsidian. I was impressed despite myself.

"It's beautiful," I said. "Nice work."

His chest swelled at the compliment. "He's a unique companion. Just don't get too close. He loves eyeballs."

Stephan laughed. He spoke to the mechanical bird, and it pushed off from his shoulder. It took flight and aimed straight for me. Right before it got within range of the sword, it made an arc, soared over my head, and went for the SUV.

CHAPTER 25

FIGHT OR FLIGHT

Mutther loomed in front of the moon, projecting his dragon shadow onto everything below as he rocketed downward. His great wings retracted against his dragon body, and then he was speeding toward the falcon.

I raced toward the drone only to see it alter its path and spin upward to meet Mutther. I froze at the sight of the bird morphing into a different shape. Its beak became a snout. Its feathers turned into scales. A long, spiked tail grew from its backside. Instead of falcon feet, it had dragon legs. The creature ascended into the clouds. Shrouded, it bellowed and blew out flames. It emerged ten times larger than it was before and continued to grow until it matched Mutther's size.

"Look out!" I shouted to Mutther, but warnings weren't necessary. Mutther took evasive action.

"You see!" Stephan yelled over the din of the dragons in flight. "My technology surpasses anything you've ever known." He laughed, gleeful at the sight of his creation. His laughter was deranged. Stephan Turner was a madman.

The ground tremors grew stronger. My allies would be here at any moment. I moved to stay between Turner and his ghosts and the SUV. We all watched the skies. Even the ghosts seemed intrigued by the impending clash of dragons.

BAM! BAM!

The dragons collided, flew apart, and collided again. Every time they smashed into each other, the drone dragon dragged its claws over Mutther's scales. Mutther deflected the worst of it, twisted his body away from the drone, and circled back around to attack from behind.

The drone dragon screeched and spit fire in random directions, searching for its attacker. Mutther was faster and zipped out of reach of its claws. Fire did nothing to Mutther's scales. He belted out his own stream of fire that blazed along the drone's back. Embers fell through the air, landing haphazardly on the ground and hitting the roof of the SUV.

From the corner of my eye, I saw Janda and Gwenn poking their heads out from the car window. Janda was wrapped in a blanket to hide her glow and was craning her neck to stare up at the sky. My pulse rose to a staccato of fear for my wife. She glanced my way and ducked back inside.

That woman was going to give me a heart attack one day.

I looked over at Stephan Turner to be sure he hadn't noticed the women. He stood with his arms crossed, his attention fixed on the ongoing battle. Now was my time to strike him down. I side-stepped my way toward him, creeping ever closer and readying my blade.

The line of ghosts noticed and moved to form a protective shield in front of him. I ground my teeth. Getting close to him was proving harder than I'd expected. If I didn't slay Turner, I'd be the one sent back to the Underworld.

The dragon battle became more intense.

I ducked when the drone dragon swooped low and set the ground ablaze as it passed by. I stumbled backward but not before my arm got singed. It was my sword arm. I clenched the sword and winced at the pain. I saw Stephan sneer through the flames that divided me and the ghosts. If I shifted, I could heal faster. But I couldn't lose the only weapon that could kill the ghosts, so I sucked in air through my nostrils and did the only thing I could to take my opponent by surprise. I found the lowest point of the divide and jumped over the wall of flames.

The fire spread along a trail of dry leaves that crackled and burned to ash behind me. The high temps warming my back became too hot, but I refused to budge. Not until I got to Stephan. He pushed several ghosts in front of him as a shield against my advance. He truly was a coward. I raised the sword and felt the tattoo sting. I swiped the blade to the left and back to the right. Any ghost in its path evaporated in a puff of smoke. Five, then eight, went up in smoke. I lost count of the number of ghosts that I sent back to Hell as I cut through Stephan's defenses.

A horse snorted in the rear of the ghost legion. The Headless Horseman had arrived. He rode his steed to the front, trampling any apparition in his path. Turner raised a fist in the air in triumph. The horseman pushed past him. I held my ground, sword raised, while my arch enemy trotted toward me. His faceless skull was a ball of fire, but in that fire were eyes black as coal staring out at me. Hatred poured off the horseman. Revenge wouldn't be enough for him. His expression told me he wanted total annihilation.

The feeling was mutual.

I couldn't face off with both Turner and the horseman. The Headless Horseman was the greater threat. I readied my sword, feeling the sting of the tattoo that let me know the magic was working. He never got off his steed. He kept coming. His horse high-stepped through the throng of ghosts. Each time a hoof landed on one, a popping sound ripped through the air as it was sent back to the Underworld. How the huge beast could do such magic defied reason. I had a weapon forged by a prince of Hell. This was a horse. What magic did it wield?

I stared in amazement at the body armor that protected the animal. I'd never been as close to it before. I knew at once the prince's smithy forged the armor and felt the touch of magic similar to mine coming from it. The hot breath of the horse's snort blasted into my face. I blinked and leaned backward.

The Headless Horseman halted when the line of ghosts faltered. Stephan was giving the ghosts commands and so was he. Except the horseman didn't shout his orders the way Turner did. No. The horseman never used his voice, but the ghosts still heard the orders.

Turner yelled at the apparitions to march toward the SUV. Some obeyed. The ones that didn't seemed lost and confused about what to do next and who to follow. I stayed out of the way and let the chaos ensue. Turner shouted at the horseman to charge at me. The horseman yanked on the reins, and his steed followed what its master demanded. No one gave orders to the Headless Horseman, not even the son of the prince of the Underworld.

He nudged his way through the ranks to reach Stephan Turner, scattering the ghost legion. Between the moonlight and the cumulative glow of the ghosts, I could see the terror on Stephan's face. He lost his bluster and fell backward onto the ground.

"Stop," he said. "You can't touch me or my father will make you pay."

The steed reared its flaming hooves above the cowering half-demon. At the last minute, the horseman pulled the reins to the left and the hooves pounded into the ground next to Turner's head—a warning about who was in charge.

The apparitions fought me the entire time the Headless Horseman put Stephan Turner in his place. As soon as the horseman returned his attention to me, Turner scrambled to his feet and dashed off into the woods.

Dammit!

I couldn't chase after Turner with ghosts surrounding me and the horseman making his way back to attack. The aerial battle took another downward direction when Mutther attempted to come to my aid. He bashed the drone sideways and banked hard to fly toward the legion and the horseman. His flight path took out the group on my left flank. As he passed, the horseman sent a volley of fire that found its mark on the underbelly of Mutther's dragon body. Mutther let out a wailing hiss of pain as he soared higher out of reach.

The sound distracted me long enough for several apparitions to launch themselves in my direction. I prepared for the impact. Sasha jumped into the fray and tore them apart, sending them back to the Underworld. Shifters poured on to the scene and began battling the otherworldly legion.

CHAPTER 26

RAINING FIRE

Ghosts, shifters, dragons, and the Headless Horseman depicted the epitome of chaos unleashed. They were all bent on defeating one another. Thankfully, my friends formed a protective ring around the SUV, with Sebastian standing guard. I saw Gwenn waving her hands out the window, making deliberate gestures as she worked one of her spells. My family would be fine. I returned my focus to the most important fight of my life.

My adversary didn't back down. This was our final stand. One of us would survive and banish the other to the dark lands of decay for eternity.

He pushed his way past his army that had scattered in front of him when Sasha attacked. He plowed through anything in his path.

A calm settled over me as I watched his approach. Sasha and the shifters kept the ghosts busy and out of my way.

CRASH!

I didn't have to look skyward to know what that sound meant. The dragons had locked talons. Each spewed fire at the other, which did nothing more than send it raining down on us. Embers landed on my arms and back, scorching the flesh. The scent of burned hair from the wolves and werecats filled the air. An enormous screech echoed around us, and the drone dragon plummeted. Mutther had ripped one of its wings. The drone could no longer navigate. Its trajectory put it squarely over the Headless Horseman, forcing him to back away. His change in direction sent his army scattering once more.

The drone dragon made a powerful thunk as it hit the pavement, causing the road to cave and buckle on impact. The brimstone eyes of the drone met my gaze before they dimmed and extinguished. One adversary down, one who ran away, and a bunch more that now followed the horseman's orders.

The ghosts kept coming. A line would fall and more filled in the gaps. Their combined energies gave them corporeal bodies that could fight us like no other opponent we'd ever encountered. Sometimes the shifters made contact and other times they slid through vapor. I took heart when the ghostly energy appeared to become more unstable. The horseman was running out of time to kill me.

We both fought against the fleeting minutes. If I didn't take him down tonight, my family would suffer immeasurable harm. More of the ghosts lost substance, making it difficult for them to engage with the shifters. I met my opponent's gaze and flashed him a grin of triumph. He roared in frustration and urged his steed to charge.

He drew nearer at an intense gallop as the demon prince's sword blazed in my grip. The weapon had yet to do the job as expected, which was to take out all my opponents. Jasper has said one sword would be enough. That wasn't happening. Hopefully, if I killed the horseman, the ghosts would retreat. I swung with renewed determination, striking the horse's armor with a sharp, resonant clang. The impact of the sword sent a jarring vibration through the horse's armor, dislodging the Headless Horseman. I saw my chance. I dropped the sword and shifted into my panther.

The feral intensity deep within me coiled, ready to strike. My human side noticed a commotion near the SUV, but my panther urged me to remain focused on my enemy. I pushed down the rising fear for my family's safety and put my faith in those I trusted to protect them.

I sprang into the air, my gaze fixed on my target. With the strength of my massive paws, I swiped at the horseman, unseating him. Both of us toppled to the ground, sending sparks flying everywhere. I sank my teeth into the flesh of his arm. The predator in me sought the usual vulnerable spot along the neck. It was a shock to learn he didn't have a neck or even much of a face. From the shoulders up, his body had no skin and little muscle or tendons. He was a decaying figure—a skeleton encased in fire.

I aimed for his heart, tearing at his chest. I wasn't sure he had a heart, either. The man he once was no longer existed. Magic kept him alive, if you could call this living. Flames seared my fur. I kept biting and clawing, but a vest of brimstone protected his heart. I couldn't defeat him, even though I'd pulled him from the vantage point of his horse, and we were in single combat. I quickly changed tactics, glancing back at the sword, gauging the distance and calculating my odds of shifting back to human to snatch it. I could shift and maybe reach the sword—maybe. Everything was riding on this new strategy.

Dammit to hell!

I went for it.

My panther twisted away from the horseman's grasp.

My muscles rippled and contorted as the transformation pushed my body to its limits. It took less than a minute for the shift back to human. That was all my enemy needed. He was on me just when my fingers touched the sword. I was dragged backward, unable to clutch the weapon. My tattoo thrummed in anticipation of being so near the sword and unable to connect with it.

Janda raced forward. She was the source of the commotion I'd heard earlier. I shouldn't have been surprised by her, but I was. Standing by while others fought was not something she could tolerate. Sebastian protected her as she advanced while Mutther shot fire into the ranks of the ghost legion to slow them down.

"No!" My cry went unheeded.

The air crackled with magic. It crackled with fiery embers. It crackled with the rage of a lykoi shifter hell-bent on protecting her mate.

She threw off the blanket covering her as she sprinted in my direction. Her radiant beauty lit the night sky like the beacon she was, causing the apparitions to pause as she darted past them. She carried our newborn daughter close to her chest. Wrenley glowed like her mother. The two combined to create a luminous display of pure power.

CHAPTER 27
VORTEX

The Headless Horseman released his hold on me and fell backward—away from the intense light emanating from Janda. Thunder roared the second she grasped the demon prince's sword. The leviathan cross, emblazoned across my chest, shot a burst of painful heat deep into my core that sent me to my knees.

"Alex!" Janda hurried toward me, one arm outstretched with the sword and the other wrapped protectively around Wrenley. The earth rumbled beside her, shaking the ground she stood on. Just as the pavement cracked, she jumped a safe distance away. The roadway fractured with the upheaval of the underlying earth that sent both shifters and ghosts scampering to escape the gaping hole expanding under their feet.

The hole became a swirling vortex of inky darkness contrasted with the reddish-orange light glowing from its depths. Heat billowed forth, and I knew what we were seeing—a lava pit like the one I'd traveled through on my journey to the demon prince's armory. This was a gateway to Hell.

Dark tendrils shaped like the serpent in the leviathan cross reached upward, seeking anything in its path and drawing it into the vortex. All our shifters retreated to the edge of the woods. Silas, Damon, and Nick gathered their shifters and ordered them to fall back.

Shock had Gwenn rooted in place. Sebastian picked her up in his arms and fled to where the others waited while Mutther circled helplessly above. Trees swayed violently back and forth. The ground shook as the air grew thick with the acrid stench of sulfur. The shadowy serpent tendrils found the nearest ghosts and dragged them down, down into the vortex's core. From deep within the depths came the heart-wrenching wails of agony and despair.

I stared at Janda in horror. The sword was being pulled toward the vortex—with Janda still holding fast to it.

"Drop it," I said, sprinting in her direction.

She stared at me in abject fear. "I can't! It won't let me go!"

I grabbed her and held on tight. I sensed the magnetic force and watched as it sucked away dozens of ghosts. The horseman wasn't immune to the effects of the swirling power of darkness. He mounted his steed, which bucked and snorted as he steered it away from the abyss. I couldn't stop him. Keeping Janda and the baby from being drawn into the vortex took all my strength.

"Take the baby," she said. "Let me go."

"No!" I refused to release my hold.

Sebastian zoomed in and wrapped his arms around my waist and tugged, pulling us a few inches from the vortex. It wasn't enough. Nick arrived and held onto Sebastian, then Silas held Nick, and Damon grabbed Silas. Finally, Gwenn grabbed Damon. He was too big for her to put her arms around his waist, so she gripped his leg. She chanted a spell of strength as more shifters joined and fought to keep Janda and the baby from being sucked away into the pit of despair that led to the Underworld. We formed a chain of supernatural creatures—shifters, vampire, witch.

I reached one hand for the sword and covered Janda's hand with mine. Her fingers loosened. I slid my hand forward, past where she gripped the sword, until I touched the hilt and it released her. She fell backward into my chest.

"It's okay, love. I'll take it from here. Get Wrenley to safety." I kissed the top of her head and with my free hand, scooted her behind me.

Sebastian grabbed her with one hand and pushed her back to Nick. They passed Janda and the baby from one person to the next until the two of them were free from the pull of the vortex.

Janda's and Wrenley's light attracted more ghosts who seemed to sense their presence. Some were smart enough to stay back, but not others. Ghosts tumbled into the vortex in droves.

The horseman held his steed at bay and watched his ghostly legion being taken from him. I glimpsed the rage pouring forth from his skull in waves of fire. He was just as helpless as I was to contain the vortex's magnetic pull.

A screech came from above us that sent shivers running down my spine. Mutther had circled and come up behind the horseman. The fierce dragon glided in low to the ground and shot flames at the horse and rider, spooking the steed. Despite the Headless Horseman's attempts to restrain it, the horse charged forward. The dragon persisted until the vortex's force ensnared the horse, and its rider pitched himself off onto the ground. The steed let out a high-pitch screech as dark tendrils pulled it into Hell's portal.

Mutther rolled his dragon body over the ground so that his opponent was trapped beneath his enormous weight. The fireballs the horseman shot at Mutther deflected off the dragon's scales. Mutther used his front legs to drag himself toward the pit, keeping the horseman pinned beneath him.

Gwenn screamed.

The dragon turned toward her scream, bowed his head as if to say goodbye, and tumbled forward into the vortex, carrying our arch enemy with him.

The serpentine tendrils shrank back within the confines of the vortex, easing slowly out of sight. Once the last tendril faded from view, the magnetic pull vanished so fast it sent our entire chain to the ground. Shifters, vampire, witch—all ended up in a heap of tangled limbs. We disengaged from one another and hurried toward the pit only to find nothing there. Dirt, gravel, pavement—gone. No more hole. No pit of darkness. No Mutther.

Gwenn fell to her knees and wept. Janda drew her into a one-armed hug while holding Wrenley, who had slept through it all. I lifted the babe from Janda's arms and helped the two women to their feet. There were no words to describe the pain of losing Mutther.

Everything around us seemed to slow and grow quiet. The remaining ghosts hovered in subdued silence. They didn't attack or even come close to Janda, yet they seemed reluctant to depart. She raised her downcast gaze to meet theirs and nodded. She walked solemnly toward them with her arms out and her palms up. The apparitions formed an orderly line and waited until she called them forward.

Janda's glow brightened in a welcoming embrace that was the complete opposite of the ominous tendrils of the vortex. The first ghost strode forward, put its hand over its heart in a sentiment of gratitude, then walked through her bright aura and disappeared. The process of allowing the ghosts to pass through the veil of death that Janda held open for them continued for close to twenty minutes. During that time, I sent several messages requesting help in locating Stephan Turner.

My fate was tied to his in the same way it had been bound to the Headless Horseman. The depth of my gratitude to Mutther for his sacrifice was beyond measure or repayment. I would watch over Gwenn and keep her safe. It was the least I could do for my friend, who had given everything to save Janda and the baby. Part of me prayed he survived and would be waiting to be brought home to us. The other part knew deep down that this was it. He would not return.

CHAPTER 28
THE AFTERMATH

As Silas and Damon tended to the wounded shifters, I asked Nick to retrieve the remnants of the dragon drone, hoping it would shed light on the workings of Stephan Turner's magical tech devices. Turner was a legit madman. He was also brilliant.

"There's not much left to it," Nick said. He held out one eyeball, a few scales, and a talon. "Sorry, man. It looks like the vortex claimed the remains. Even the road showed little sign of damage. The damn pit was like a Hoover vacuum. Take a look around us. It's like nothing happened. That's some crazy shit."

I scanned the area, noting a few broken tree branches and a bunch of scorches along uneven pavement that could have been from a kid doing burnouts with his car. We knew better what caused the marks, but it wasn't likely to raise the brows of any passing motorists once daylight came. That was about the extent of the destruction.

"Yeah. Crazy."

"What do you want me to do with this tech stuff?" He

rolled the eyeball around in his palm. "It's not squishy. It's hard like stone."

"Maybe Sid can tell us more about it. But it's definitely made of brimstone." I tapped the eyeball with my finger. "It doesn't seem activated. It's dull and dark, like the kind that's mined in the Underworld before it's infused with demon magic."

Nick froze. "You sure it's safe to handle?"

"It should be." When I saw his body stiffen, I tried to dispel his unease. "Yeah. Don't worry about it. Nothing is going to happen to you."

"Very reassuring, Alex. Remind me to not ask you to do any pep talks with the shifters." He closed his hand over the remains of the drone. "I'll take it to Sid now. The sooner I can get rid of it, the better."

"On your way, could you tell everyone to head home? I'll be at Sebastian's with Janda and the baby if anyone needs me." I glanced at Gwenn. "We'll bring Gwenn with us, too."

He followed my gaze to Gwenn being comforted by Janda. "Do you think he's dead?" His voice was rough with pain.

I sighed. "I do."

"But we're talking about Mutther here. That dude is indestructible, right?" Nick's eyes held a glimmer of hope.

"I don't know. But we have friends in the Underworld who can help us search for him."

We could trust Maude to send her people out to scout the area around the Underworld town. However, if Mutther had ended up in the demon prince's territory, then we would have a harder time gathering reliable intel. And if Mutther truly landed in Hell, the domain of Jasper's father, then we were screwed. In that case, it would be better for

Mutther if he was really dead and had passed over the river that I'd traversed, carrying souls to the other side.

"Speaking of Underworld friends, where's that dog you brought back?"

"Shit. I don't know." I surveyed the area to no avail. "Sasha's gone. I hope she's not causing mischief somewhere."

"Do you think she got sucked into the vortex?"

"I hope not. But she's a free spirit, so she may have simply taken off." The thought of a magical dog roaming around Sleepy Hollow was one more thing to add to my growing list of concerns.

"She's good to have around," he said. "Maybe she'll turn up."

"Maybe," I said. "She sure helped us out tonight. Like you did with saving my ass. Thanks for that. We would have met the same fate as Mutther if it hadn't been for you."

"Nah. It was tug-of-war against the vortex. We all played our part."

"Then I'm glad I was on the winning team."

"Me, too."

He lumbered off to pass along the word about going home. His step was heavy. His shoulders slumped. Most of the shifters stopped over to offer condolences to Gwenn before leaving. She accepted their kindness with a nod of thanks.

Sorry.

We're here for you.

Praying for you.

Once the last of the shifters departed, Gwenn collapsed into Janda's arms. Wrenley awoke, and her tiny hands reached up and touched Gwenn's hair, leaving behind a trail of soft light. I gasped. I'd never seen anything like it. Janda heard me and met my gaze. Gwenn's prediction that the baby would be gifted had been right.

Janda handed the baby to Gwenn, who took comfort in holding Wrenley.

Sebastian came to stand by me and watched Wrenley. "She's amazing, like her mother."

"Yes, she is," I said. "Let's just hope the chaos that follows wherever Janda goes doesn't follow Wrenley."

"Good luck with that one," he said. "I'm going to see how the Mercedes fared so we can get these girls home. You and I will figure out what to do about Stephan Turner later."

He strode off to examine his SUV.

The sword hung limply in my hand. I hadn't even realized I was still holding the weapon. It no longer glowed, or made my leviathan cross burn. Had the magic embedded in the sword disappeared? The horseman was back where he belonged, but not Turner. I rubbed the tattoo. It damn well better disappear once I fulfilled my deal. My head ached now that the battle had ended and my family was safe. I pressed my fingers to my temple as if that might ease the throbbing.

Mutther was our only casualty, which was a blessing considering how vicious the fighting had been. We had quite a few non-life-threatening injuries that would heal relatively fast once the shifters got some rest. Considering everything, we'd done well. But losing Mutther was indescribable. It was devastating to our entire shifter community. I didn't want to ponder what might have happened to him. I had to keep my shit together. My agreement with Jasper was only half-finished. I still had to hunt down his son and get Stephan back to the Underworld.

The guy was a piece of work. He was smart, shifty, and a survivor.

I tried to put myself in his place and think of what I'd do if I had every in town after me. Then I realized that's what it was like when I was in the Underworld. My hidden home had provided me with refuge. I'd bet anything Stephan Turner also had a hideout. I just had to find it.

CHAPTER 29

CONFESSION

As soon as we'd gotten everyone settled, Sebastian brought the doctor he had retained for the birth to the house. The doctor was kind and efficient. Despite being human, he had been around Sleepy Hollow for decades and was well-versed in its supernatural residents. His examination of the baby and Janda was thorough. He recommended Janda take a day or two off to rest. I could tell from her expression that she had no intention of following that advice. To my immense relief, Wrenley was in perfect health. He also examined Gwenn for shock. He suggested warm blankets, some hot tea, and some rest. She refused the sedatives he offered.

The doctor cooed at Wrenley while he packed his medical bag to leave. "Congratulations, Alex and Janda. Your daughter is magnificent. I can't wait to see how her talents evolve."

"She's bound to keep her parents busy," Sebastian said. "She's the spitting image of her mother and, I dare say, has her mother's unique gifts, judging by how they lit up the night sky tonight."

Gwenn smiled. "I told you the baby would be special." Her voice didn't have its usual upbeat tone, but she was trying. That was all we could expect after she lost Mutther.

The doctor kneeled in front of Gwenn, who was sitting at a small dining table, and checked her pulse one more time. "Everything seems normal. Try to rest, and don't hesitate to call me if you need anything. Again, I'm sorry for your loss."

"That's very kind of you," Gwenn said.

Sebastian walked the doctor out. Gwenn's body sagged. I handed her the cup of soothing herbal tea Sebastian had made. Who knew the old vampire could make tea? I waited for him to return before broaching the topic weighing on my mind. He came back while I was holding Wrenley.

He kissed the baby's head and trailed a finger along her delicate cheek. "No one is ever going to hurt you, little one. Uncle Sebastian will rip their throats out if they try. Okay?"

"That's great, Sebastian. Just give the baby nightmares, why don't you?" I gave the baby back to Janda.

"You should know by now that I don't lie. I *will* destroy anyone who attempts to harm this child." He made to leave the room but paused. "I'll be in my study."

"Wait," Janda said. "Did you just mark Wrenley?"

He shrugged. "What if I did?"

She grinned. "In this instance, it's fine. You have my blessing to do so."

He inclined his head in her direction. "Thank you."

I was on board with the marking as well, fully understanding its importance and willing to accept all the help I could find to keep my daughter safe. She might need it, especially if something happened to me and I ended up back in the Underworld. I hadn't told them about the clock ticking away the minutes of my time with my family.

"Sebastian, could you stay for a moment? I have something to share with all of you." I glanced at Janda. Her gaze narrowed.

"What did you do?" she said.

The air grew instantly cooler around us. It may have been my imagination, but I didn't think so. My wife seemed to emit a frosty vibe that affected the energy in the space. Perfect. I was in trouble already and hadn't even explained my problem.

"Me? I did the same thing you did not long ago. I made a deal with the devil's son."

"You didn't." She was *not* happy.

Sebastian glared at me. Gwenn raised a brow, and Hudson, who had been napping this whole time, raised his head and hissed.

"Give me a break," I said. "I went to the Underworld for weapons to use against the ghosts. What did you think would happen? Did you think Jasper would just hand over a magical sword?"

Janda shifted Wrenley to nurse her. "Sorry. No throwing stones at glass houses from me. Continue."

"Thank you." I paced the floor, searching for the best way to confess what I'd agreed to do. Yeah. I had nothing.

"Spit it out," Sebastian said. "And stop pacing. You're annoying me."

I paused and met Janda's gaze. "In hindsight, I should have told you, but the result would have been the same, and I didn't want to worry you. I'm sorry."

Janda was scowling.

I took a breath and continued my narrative. "Jasper wants his kid back in the Underworld. That was his number-one demand. The horseman was his other demand. In fact, it wouldn't surprise me if the Headless Horseman was in chains as we speak."

"You already told us this," Sebastian said.

"Yes. Yes, I did. There is one catch. I have three days to complete the task or forfeit my life to the service of the demon prince as his new smithy. I'm on day two now."

The silence that followed made my skin prickle. Oh, man. I had done it this time.

Janda got out of the recliner, where she'd been sitting comfortably with Wrenley. She swaddled the baby and came up to me. Instead of smacking some God-given sense into me, she kissed me. I blinked.

"Okay," she said. "Time is wasting. What do we do?"

And that was the woman I fell in love with—her love, loyalty, and fierce protectiveness defining the depth of our connection.

"Mutther didn't sacrifice himself for nothing," Gwenn said. "Count me in."

"And me, as well," Sebastian said. "Finding Stephan Turner is our top priority."

"Agreed," Gwenn added. "But what happens when you find him? How do you deliver him to Jasper?"

I retrieved the sword from the umbrella stand outside the room. I knew better than to bring it inside the nursery. Gwenn was adamant it didn't cross the threshold to the baby's room, so I stood in the doorway with it. "This didn't work the way Jasper claimed it would. But supposedly, if I slay Turner with it, then he'll be transported back to the Underworld, or so Jasper said. I'm not sure that's true, since he also said I'd only need one sword to defeat all the ghosts. Well, we see how that turned out."

Gwenn met me at the door and inspected the sword. "Alex, it did do exactly what Jasper said it would." She turned to stare at Janda and Wrenley. "If I'm not mistaken, the demon prince expected Janda to use the sword. Alex, it wasn't designed for *you* to take out all the ghosts. It was designed for Janda."

"That bastard," I said. My panther stirred, as pissed off as I was, and wanting to retaliate against Jasper.

Janda came to the hall and stared at the sword without touching it. "He'd been trying to reach me through my dreams, but I kept blocking him. He used Alex to get me to do what he wanted."

"He used both of you," Sebastian said, joining us in the hall. "He knew the bond you share and what you'd sacrifice for one another. But what he didn't consider was what others would be willing to sacrifice on your behalf. The magic in the sword wasn't enough to conquer such an adversary. He knew that and assumed Janda would come to your aid, which she did."

My pulse rate rocketed. "He expected her to touch the sword. You're saying that he created a device that would open a portal to the Underworld only when she grabbed it?" I ground my teeth. "I was the one he assumed would take the horseman through the vortex. It should have been me and not Mutther."

Gwenn touched my arm. "He fulfilled his destiny. It was in Mutther's genetic code as an Uther dragon to protect at all costs. I was aware this day would come, and so was Mutther. It doesn't mean it doesn't hurt."

I pulled her into a brief hug and released her. "I'm sorry."

"Sorry is for those who don't try. You saved Janda from being transported to the Underworld," she said. "I'm sure Jasper would have loved for her to be sucked in. He wouldn't mind having her by his side."

"Not happening," Janda said. "Alex, where do we find Stephan Turner?" Her determination raised my spirits. Maybe I could complete my contract with Jasper.

"He's hiding where he thinks he's safe," I said.

Sebastian tugged his cape around his shoulders. "Why are we standing here in the hall? If you know where to find him, let's go."

"First, Sid is the one who can help locate him. Second, you will not go after him without me being there. Turner is a half-demon. He has magical tech that could destroy us all. It's going to take more than fangs, vampire or shifter, to bring this guy down. It's going to take activating the sword again, and maybe the vortex."

CHAPTER 30

REVERSING MAGIC

Sebastian tossed me the car keys to the Mercedes SUV. "Here. It's yours. I figured Wrenley claimed it the moment Janda gave birth to her. I'll have it put in Janda's name this week."

She gave him a peck on the cheek. "Thanks, Uncle Sebastian."

"*Humph.* You can stop calling me 'uncle.' That's reserved for Wrenley." He slid into the front passenger seat, but not before tucking a blanket over Wrenley, who had once again fallen asleep.

Janda secured the car seat and sat next to the baby. Gwenn took the seat beside Janda, and Hudson jumped up on Gwenn's lap. He'd become glued to her side ever since she got back from assisting with Wrenley's birth. They'd left Hudson at Sebastian's house when Gwenn hopped onto Mutther's dragon for the flight to meet us on the roadside. Hudson let it be known he was not happy with any of us. I had a feeling he would not let Gwenn out of his sight for quite some time. Hopefully, he didn't mind dogs, because Sasha might show up when least expected.

I drove to Sid's warehouse and parked at the top level of his garage. We didn't pass a single vehicle after we drove onto his property. Apparently, Sid had cleared out the building when I messaged him we were on our way. Normally, by this hour of the early evening, his place was filling up with a plethora of gamers.

The elevator was filled to capacity with a vampire, a witch with a tag-along cat, and two shifters with a newborn who may or may not be a shifter. Wrenley had shown her witch heritage, but only time would tell if she was a shifter.

The cameras panned the occupants of the elevator, pausing a moment on Sebastian then swiveling back into place. The hidden door slid open to reveal Sid at his work-table, surrounded by the parts of the downed drone. He waved us toward him.

"Come in. Come in," he said. "This is exciting shit, Alex. Very exciting. Wait until you get a load of what our man Turner has been up to." He beamed from ear to ear.

"Holy guacamole!" Gwenn said, putting Hudson on the cement floor and surveying the myriad of security moni-tors. "Sid, you have an interesting setup here. Your hidden front door is especially cool."

He seemed self-conscious of the attention. "Thanks. It's not much, but it's home."

Janda put the infant car seat on a couch that looked like it also served as Sid's bed. A pillow and several blankets had been shoved to one side. Wrenley was asleep and making what sounded like tiny purrs.

We gathered around Sid and the array of tech he'd spread out on the table. I propped the sword against a table leg. "What did you find out?"

Sid's eyes glistened with delight. "Okay. We know

Stephan Turner swiped magic-infused brimstone from his father, right?"

"Yeah. That's the impression I got. So?" I wasn't sure where he was going with this but kept an open mind.

"Come on, Alex. Think. You made the sword. What did you learn while forging it?" Sid tapped his fingers on the table. "What makes the sword and this drone work?"

"Brimstone," Janda said. "Oh. My. God." She glanced at my tattoo.

"What?" Gwenn said.

Sid poked the leviathan cross. "This, my friend, is the answer you seek. Infused brimstone powers Turner's tech, but something has to unlock the power to activate it. Think of the brimstone as the lock and your tattoo as a key."

Sebastian picked up the deactivated eyeball made of brimstone. "It's a link to the Underworld?"

Sid clapped his hands. "Yes!"

"Shit," I said. "No wonder Jasper wants his kid back. Turner stole brimstone, but as Jasper's son, he also has the ability to manipulate it."

"Exactly!" Sid was bouncing on his feet. He was like a kid at Christmas, giddy and squirmy all at once.

Hudson meowed and rubbed against Gwenn. "Oh, yes, Hudson. That could be true," she said.

We all stared at the cat, who was communicating with Gwenn. She perked up at whatever Hudson had told her. She went to where the sword lay against the wooden table leg. "May I?"

I shrugged. "Sure. It should be safe to handle. If it was active, I'd feel it in my tattoo."

She placed the sword next to the dragon drone eye. "Hudson has the idea that there's more than one key that's needed to open the doorway to the Underworld. Alex could wield the sword against his paranormal foes, but that was one level of its magic. You could say that the tattoo was the first key."

The drone eye glimmered with faint light. Gwenn put the sword even closer to it. The eye's pupil widened, and the iris glowed a light yellow. My tattoo ached but didn't sting. I grabbed the sword and moved it away from the brimstone eye. The glow dimmed and vanished.

"*That* was interesting," Sebastian said. "Unfortunately, Gwenn, I see a flaw in your theory of the vortex. Janda was holding the sword when the vortex opened. Alex didn't touch it until *after* the vortex opened."

"True, but Sid is correct," she said. "It takes two keys to open the vortex. As a traveler, Janda is a natural key, because she can create pathways into the Underworld."

"That only works for spirits," Janda said.

"Not when you opened the vortex," Gwenn said. "We can agree that the sword is a lock and Janda is a key, just as the tattoo that Jasper placed on Alex is a key. Alex was not in contact with the sword for his tattoo to activate it as the second key. But there was someone else who was near Janda."

"No!" Janda spun to look at Wrenley, sound asleep in her car seat. "Are you saying that the baby is a key?"

Gwenn strode over to sit next to Wrenley. "That's exactly what I'm suggesting. Think about it. Stephan Turner was born in the Underworld. Wrenley was conceived in the Underworld, and she's the daughter of a traveler."

"Dammit," I said. "Keep the sword away from Wrenley. We don't want a vortex opening up."

"It won't," Sid said. "Gwenn is pretty spot on. It takes a

combination of keys and a special lock. After experimenting with the drone pieces, I think the brimstone magic may have a lifespan. The talon and the piece of dragon scale glowed when I held them next to the original drone that Shawn had signed out of the evidence locker. Now, the talon does nothing, and neither does the original device. That could be why Stephan Turner wanted to reach the peak of his tech prowess pronto. It's my guess he's running out of the brimstone he stole from his demon father. The stone is like a rechargeable battery. You can only charge it a limited number of times before you have to get a new battery."

I moved the sword to the other side of the room, well away from Wrenley and Janda. "That doesn't make me feel better, Sid. How the hell do we know when the magic is drained? Sorry. Can't risk it."

"I hear you. Trust me, I get it," Sid said. "That's not the only reason I asked you to come over. I believe we can reverse-engineer the magic to help us defeat Turner." Sid puttered with the drone pieces until he'd successfully opened the dragon scale. Inside the scale was a tiny circuit board.

"Now, I've only just started to mess with this tech," he said, "but I've been studying Turner for a while and know some of what to expect. For all his claims about emerging technology, he's actually old school in his hardware. If we can tweak the circuitry, we may be able to use this to track Turner. The biggest issue is distance. We'd have to be within a mile or less for it to ping Turner's location. That's also assuming Turner has the cell phone he used to give voice commands to his drones."

"You're kidding? Here I thought Turner was whispering magic words into the drone to give it commands, and you're saying he was using his phone?" I felt pretty stupid for falling for Turner's theatrics.

Sid put the dragon scale to one side and began trying to pry open the eye. "Oh, I'm sure he put on a good show, whispering into the drone. He has a flare for drama. It keeps him in the tech limelight. It also works well for him on the prankster site. People believe the crap he spews and end up being avid followers who will do anything to get close to the guy who proclaims to have the next great invention."

"I must admit to being rather amazed by the drones he used in battle," Sebastian said. "The falcon-turned-dragon was particularly impressive."

"I'm with Sebastian," Janda said. "I don't care what the guy used to make his devices. That's like nothing I've ever seen before."

"Well," Sid said, "I'm fairly confident I've managed to adjust the settings so the brimstone eye will light up when it's near the source of its power, which would be the supply of brimstone Turner is using. Unfortunately, I couldn't tell you where to search for him."

"I think I can help with that," I said. "What do you know about the prankster site?"

Sid rubbed a hand under his chin. "Not much. Turner is clever to use a dummy account to run the forum. I've sent what I know to Shawn. There are at least a half dozen leads for where Turner might have a hidden sanctuary based on the chatter on the prankster site. The police have been busy following the leads. You'd have to touch base with Shawn to see if anything useful popped up."

As if Shawn had a sixth sense about me wanting to reach him, my phone buzzed. I glanced at the message and breathed a sigh of relief. "Shawn says they found Turner's car a few miles from one of Sid's leads, but Turner wasn't anywhere around. They're going to investigate the house where he might be hiding." I glanced at the people in the room. "We may have our chance soon to test Sid's theory."

"Finally, some good news," Janda said.

"Don't take this the wrong way, love, but I can't risk losing you and the baby. You both were almost sucked into the vortex. The demon prince would love to have you under his roof, and all the better to have Wrenley there, too. Sorry. You're staying here." There was no way Janda was coming with us to face Turner.

CHAPTER 31

CATCH ME IF YOU CAN

When Janda was silent and not arguing about something I've said that I knew she wouldn't like, I got worried. I kept giving her furtive glances. She ignored me. Wrenley woke up and demanded to be fed. Janda changed the baby's diaper and breastfed her. Within minutes, the baby went back to sleep. Janda didn't glance my way once. I was in the doghouse, but worse, I had no idea what my wife was plotting.

My phone buzzed repeatedly. Shawn kept me in the loop as they followed several trails that might lead to Turner's location.

"Dammit," I said, reading the most recent text. "Shawn says they lost Turner's trail. The place was empty and scrubbed clean. They couldn't even get a full fingerprint. They're putting some men on surveillance duty in case he shows up."

I hated to do it, but I had to go with my original plan. "Gwenn, do you think you could try scrying again? I realize it's difficult after losing Mutther, but it would help if you could try. All we need is a general area, and then we can use the reverse tech Sid created to home in on Turner."

She bit her lip and didn't answer right away. After a long minute, she nodded.

"I'll give it a shot." She went over to where Sid was still tinkering with the eyeball. "Do you think I could borrow one of the drone pieces?"

Her unexpected appearance in his tech-nerd bubble caught him off guard. "Oh. Umm sure. Which one do you want? The eyeball?"

She made a face at the suggestion. "No. You keep it. Maybe the scale?"

He handed the dragon scale to her. "All yours. Good luck."

She took the piece and headed back toward the couch. "Thanks. Let's hope we have better luck with this than we did with the original drone."

Sebastian dimmed the light in the room. I borrowed a bowl and filled it with water, which I placed on the coffee table. Gwenn placed the drone dragon scale next to the bowl. Janda and Gwenn sat on the floor, holdings hands, and chanting their witch spell. Sid put aside his work and came to watch. The dragon scale in front of Gwenn began to spin. I sucked in my breath as it whirled, first one way and then the next.

Gwenn's eyes rolled back, and she spoke slowly in a deep voice. "Catch me if you can."

The water flew upward from the bowl and splashed back down, spraying droplets everywhere. Gwenn's head slumped forward. Janda grabbed her and laid her gently on the floor. She rubbed vigorously along Gwenn's arms and pressed her hand over Gwenn's forehead.

"That wasn't supposed to happen," Janda said, staring up at me. She smoothed dark curls of hair out of Gwenn's eyes. "Gwenn. Can you hear me? Come back. Follow the sound of my voice."

This was a crisis I had little experience with and felt utterly helpless. I hovered over the women and said a silent prayer. Mutther would kill me if anything happened to Gwenn.

A few minutes passed, and Gwenn was still out cold.

"Should we call the doctor?" I said.

Janda shook her head. "No. Give her time. The color is coming back in her face. She's had too many shocks for one night. This takes a lot of energy to recover from a possession."

"A possession?" Sebastian's voice resounded around the open warehouse space.

Janda shushed him. "You'll wake the baby."

"Sorry," he said, leaning closer and lowering his voice. "What do you mean, a possession?"

"Just what I said. Someone spoke through her."

I dropped to my knees next to Gwenn. "It's Stephan Turner. He's taunting us."

Hudson, being the helpful cat that he was, plunked himself on Gwenn's chest and hissed whenever we tried to move him. He purred and nuzzled Gwenn's chin.

When he started kneading at her shirt, Gwenn opened her eyes. "Get off, you silly kitty," she said.

Hudson meowed once and hopped off to strut away like the hero he thought he was to his beloved mistress.

I helped Gwenn sit up. "Take it easy. Go slow or you might pass out."

She gave me a smidgeon of a smile. "I'll be fine." She

smacked her lips together. "I feel all cotton mouth. Could I get something to drink?"

Sid rushed to bring her a drink, handing it to her and stepping back. She took a gulp and gasped, choking on the liquid. "This isn't water." Her voice was rough and raspy.

The expression on Sid's face was of complete confusion. "Of course it's not. It's vodka. Why would I give you water?"

"You idiot," I said. "The woman just collapsed, and you want to give her booze? What were you thinking?"

He shrugged. "I thought that's what you did when people pass out. I don't have smelling salts and figured vodka would be the next best thing."

He honestly didn't see anything wrong with what he'd done. I shook my head in disbelief at how someone so damn smart could lack common sense.

"It's fine," Gwenn said. "Thanks, Sid. I just need a minute, and some water, please." She was regaining her ability to speak now that the initial burn of the vodka passed.

Sid dutifully brought her a bottle of water, which she took several gulps of before breathing normally again.

Janda sat back on her heels. "You gave us a fright. What happened?"

"I don't know," Gwenn said. "Everything was fine, like it usually is when scrying, but then I caught a glimpse of Stephan Turner. It was as if he stood next to us in this room. It was weird. He knew I was watching. He looked straight at me and smiled. There's something wrong with that man."

"You're telling me," I said. "He used the channel you created to get a message to me."

"That's the demon in him," Sid said. He glanced at the dragon scale. It was still spinning but much more slowly. "What do you make of that?"

Gwenn pulled herself over to the coffee table, watching the scale. She glanced up at Sid. "You did it. You created a device to detect Turner's presence. He may not have been here physically, but his energy came through, and the device is letting us know about Turner's presence."

"That's good to know," Sebastian said. "It doesn't tell us where to find him, though."

Gwenn stood on wobbly legs. I put my hand out to support her, but she waved off my help. "Thanks. I really am fine. Sid, do you have a pad of paper and pencil I could use?"

Sid dashed off to retrieve the items. "Here you go." He handed them to her. "Sorry about the vodka."

"Don't worry about it. Your heart was in the right place." She took the pencil and began drawing a building surrounded by trees and a water tank.

"I know that spot," I said.

"You should," Janda said. "We've run through the Rockefeller Preserve loads of times after shifting. Gwenn, is this where Turner is located?"

"He may have used me to get a message to Alex, but the channel works both ways. Yes. He's somewhere in that area." She turned to Sid. "Get your magical detector device ready. I think it's time we used it."

Sid rubbed his hands together. "Yes! Give me a minute, and I'll have it ready to go."

My plan to trap Stephan Turner had turned into a hunting party. "Whoa, whoa, whoa. Hold up. This is not a group adventure. We are not all going. This guy is a dangerous demon."

"Half-demon," Janda said. "And we *are* all going. Unless you prefer to stay here and we go without you." She crossed her arms over her chest. "Your choice."

I groaned in defeat. "Tell me again why I married you?"

Janda smirked. "Because you can't live without me."

"True," I said. "Okay. Pack it up, everyone. We have a half-demon to catch."

CHAPTER 32

Hunting Adventure

"This isn't how I want our daughter to grow up," I said, driving the car out of Sid's garage and onto the main road.

"We're Sleepy Hollow Hunters, Alex. What did you think it would be like?" Janda said, then cooed to Wrenley. "Don't mind him, baby. Daddy's a cranky panther butt."

We had a few miles to go before reaching the Rockefeller Preserve where we'd meet the wolf and panther shifters. Other than a quick nap, Janda hadn't slept. I wasn't much better. My source of fuel was pure rage. We sent messages to Damon, Nick, and Silas, requesting backup for the encounter with Turner, assuming we found him.

A lot was riding on Gwenn's information and Sid's modifications to the drone parts. Having Wrenley with us presented a whole set of new problems. Fatherhood had just started, and I was already unsure of my decisions. A baby on a hunt. This had to be child endangerment. Thankfully, shifters had different rules than humans regarding such things.

Wrenley purred.

"Did you hear that?" Janda said, smiling like a proud momma. "I do believe we have a shifter in the family."

"A witch shifter," Gwenn corrected.

"Alex, you have a cool family," Sid said. He was all the way in the back bench seat and still tinkering with his equipment.

"Yes, he does," Sebastian said.

"Thanks." I pressed my foot to the gas and picked up speed. My family was growing in leaps and bounds to include more than my wife and child. I glanced over at Sebastian, who rode shotgun. "Why are you riding in the car? I thought you preferred using your vampire tricks to travel faster."

"For your information, I enjoy riding in cars," Sebastian said. "Why do you think I have such a vast collection of vehicles? Besides, you need me to keep Wrenley safe while you and Janda rip Stephan Turner to pieces and send his body parts back to his demon father, who can take the rest of eternity to put him back together again."

"Right." There was no arguing with Sebastian's logic. That was exactly what I had in mind for Turner. Jasper only said to kill his son. He didn't specify how. I was thinking I'd use the sword, which took up yet more space in the cramped car, to slice and dice the bastard. Then I'd toss the parts into the vortex and send the sword in after him. Jasper could keep his magic weapon.

I had my kind of magic. It was called family.

Nighttime in Rockefeller Preserves had always been fun for my clan and also for the wolf packs. The Accords for the supernatural community that Sebastian helped to create had solidified our friendship with all the paranormals in Sleepy Hollow. Those bonds were more important than ever as we worked together to fight a common foe—Stephan Turner.

Ignoring the "closed at dusk" sign, I drove into the preserve and stopped about a mile from the tank that provided water for the town. The monumental tank, capable of holding over 880,000 gallons of water, had been cleverly built so only the rim was visible. A wall had been constructed around it using the stone recovered from the original structure. If I were looking for a place to hide, or to ambush someone trying to catch me, I'd pick this location. The trees were bountiful and the foliage dense. Perfect to see without being seen.

I pulled the car over and got out, sniffing the air for any unusual scents. I found none. We were the first to arrive, so I had time to do a little reconnaissance.

"Please stay here while I scout the area leading to the tank." I stared directly at Janda. "Please."

She grumbled to make sure I got the point that I was being unfair and overprotective. I knew she must be itching to shift after having Wrenley, but now wasn't the time. If I made it out of this alive, I'd take her for a couple's run.

Sebastian scanned the area and herded the women closer to the SUV. Janda couldn't object, since Wrenley woke up and started fussing. Janda had to keep her quiet, and nursing the baby did the job of keeping our bundle of joy from alerting anyone to our presence as well as making sure Janda stayed put. It was a win-win for me, although I knew I'd hear about it once we were alone.

I removed my clothes and tossed them on the front seat to retrieve later then shifted to allow my panther free rein to explore. If there were traps, we needed to know. I didn't want anyone else getting hurt on my behalf. I noticed an area that had been trampled, so I bent down and inhaled deeply, trying to discern the scents. Again, there weren't many.

Fall leaves were already beginning to drop, making stealth more difficult. I'd been at it for less than five minutes when I heard faint footsteps behind me and knew immediately I'd been followed.

"Hey," Janda whispered.

It wasn't not easy rolling my eyes at someone while in my panther form, but I must have done a pretty decent job, judging by the disgusted look she gave me.

She sighed. "Really? You're going to be like that? I left the baby with Gwenn so I could bring you this."

She unwrapped a handkerchief I recognized as Sebastian's, revealing the eyeball Sid had been working on. He must have finished the reversal magic he'd been telling us about. I did a quick survey of our surroundings and shifted back. She brought me the clothes I'd left in the SUV. She also had the sword by her side. I was not happy.

I hastily donned my clothes and took the sword from her. "Why did you bring this?"

"Hello? You'll want to have it if you come upon Turner."

"That's correct, except I was planning to scout the area and go back to get it."

"Just think of it as me saving you a trip. You can have this, too."

She gave me the eyeball, handkerchief included. The eye had a light yellowish glow to it. I inspected it and glanced at her. "It's glowing."

It was her turn to roll her eyes. "Yes, it is. That's why I followed you. Now you can use it to detect Turner's brimstone and, hopefully, Turner." She spoke each word slowly to make her point clear.

"Thanks," I said. I watched the ground to see if it would open beneath us. "No vortex."

She nodded. "Sid is pretty smart. He told me I could carry it without fear of opening a vortex as long as I didn't touch it and the sword. He also thinks it wouldn't open after the circuit-board modifications he did on the eye. We decided not to take any chances, and he wrapped it up to keep it from coming in contact with my skin." She shrugged. "Nothing has happened, so I guess he was right."

I knew when to give up, and now was that time. "Since you're here, we might as well keep going before the eyeball magic fades like it did in the other pieces." I held the glowing device out in front of me."

Janda stared as its light intensified.

My anxiety spiked having her with me. "I'm not sure the sword alone will do the job. Changing the circuitry means we won't have two keys to use for us to create a new vortex." This was tricky. My plan to use one of the devices, along with my tattoo, had evaporated. The universe was conspiring to get Janda involved, and I hated it. Fighting Turner and keeping my wife safe at the same time had my stomach in knots.

"We're a team, remember?" she said. "I know you don't want me to get sucked away. I'm with you there. Don't worry. We'll figure it out."

I had to admire her confidence. She was an impressive bounty hunter who was in her element. "Let's hope that Jasper wasn't lying about the sword sending his son back to the Underworld."

"Jasper doesn't lie," she said. "He omits details, like the vortex, but he doesn't consider that lying."

The light in the eyeball intensified when I faced west. It decreased when I turned east. "West it is. Stay close."

I didn't know if a half-demon had heightened senses but took care to stay quiet as we drew closer to our target. Janda was a seasoned hunter. There was no need to remind her to do the same. The rest of the shifters would be here soon, if they weren't already with Sebastian. However, my gut told me not to wait.

We wound our way past the trees leading to the water tank. The eyeball got so bright that I had to shove it in my pocket to keep from giving our position away. We'd hit the mark. Jasper's dwindling stash of brimstone was nearby. He would be, too. You don't leave your source of magical power unattended for long. Turner was a man on the run. He wouldn't be able to lie low for long. Cornering him would bring out his demon and force him to make a stand. He wouldn't go willingly back to the Underworld. I couldn't blame him. It was a dismal place to live. Jasper wasn't the type to make life easy for a kid who stole from him. Heck, Jasper knew exactly what it was like to be punished by your old man, and Turner had seen how unforgiving his family was for screwing up. No. Stephan Turner would go down fighting.

I paused to listen and froze.

Humans were ambling around the tank that stood about five hundred yards from us. Stephan Turner may no longer have his massive ghost legion, but he had dozens of humans following him like he was a God about to bestow his blessings on them.

This was bad.

Janda tugged on my arm and pointed toward the left side of the structure, where the wall curved around the massive tank. Stephan Turner strode out into the open.

"I know you're here, Alex. Join me." Turner spread his arms wide in a welcoming gesture.

He stared straight ahead as if he knew where we were. We had been in that spot earlier but had moved. My guess was he had some surveillance cameras that he had been viewing from the other side of the tank. As soon as he stepped forward, he no longer knew our exact position. At least, that was what I hoped.

I motioned for Janda to stay hidden then circled back around in the direction he was gazing. I stood and walked out into the open to meet him.

CHAPTER 33

SHOWDOWN

"There you are, Alex," Turner said.

He had a wide grin on his face that didn't match the malice in his eyes. He lowered his arms and took one step back. That seemed to be a signal for his followers to gather behind him. Men and women of various statures grouped together to form a line of defense for their leader. As humans, they lacked the keen sight of shifters or demons to see well at night. I also wasn't sure how much demon was in Turner or what his demonic powers might be. Jasper never alluded to him having any.

Several of the humans held lanterns that gave the area an eerie glow but allowed them to see me. Turner gazed past where I stood.

"It's just me," I said, "for now. But you better decide fast whether you'll go willingly back to your father."

He glanced at the sword I held in my right hand. I moved it away from my side for him to get a really good look and also to position it better for me to strike.

"Jasper sent you to fetch me and gave you a sword. How nice of him."

The sour expression on his face told me just how much he hated his father. He moved to stand in line with the first row of followers, who spread apart enough to give him space to join them.

"I wouldn't know about how nice he is," I said. "I do know he is true to his word, despite manipulating the terms of his contracts. It's you or me, Turner, and I want it to be you."

That was all he needed to hear. He spread open his long coat to reveal a multitude of pockets within its lining. Inside each was a glowing object. Turner was wearing his stash of brimstone, which made him the perfect second key. My leviathan tattoo warmed beneath my shirt. If I could get within striking range, the sword would do its job and a vortex would open to send Stephan Turner back to the Underworld.

"Nice coat," I said. "You thought of that all by yourself, did you?" I was goading him and stalling for time. I couldn't defeat dozens of attackers, even if they were humans. My plan to confront Turner didn't account for his new recruits. I needed backup.

Janda's lykoi padded over to my side. I stiffened. How was I going to protect her against this mob and keep her from being sucked into a vortex? Then I remembered a mamma bear could be extraordinarily lethal if she felt her cubs were threatened in any way. My wife was that mamma bear. She let out a guttural sound that made even my arm hairs stand on end. I smiled when several of the crowd flinched.

"My wife isn't too happy with you, Turner. You threatened her baby, even before she was born, when you sent your moronic prankster guys after her. She doesn't take kindly to that sort of thing."

I placed my left hand on Janda's furry neck. Lykoi cats were a rare breed of shifters. They possessed elements of both cat and wolf. A good bit of her was covered in thin cat hairs—except around her face. The fur around her eyes and cheeks gave her a true wolf's appearance. Janda wasn't just any shifter, either. Her witch heritage as a traveler had been growing in strength, making her a deadly adversary. I had to prayed it would be enough to keep her out of range of the vortex I intended to create.

Her presence made the group antsy. Just as Turner withdrew one of his drones, a guy produced a gun. He aimed it at Janda. Turner let the drone loose, and it flew into the air toward us. The bigger concern was the trigger-happy idiot facing us. I raised the sword and moved in front of Janda, bracing for the impact of the bullet. But before the guy could pull the trigger, Sasha mowed him down with her swift attack.

The man screamed. "No! Get it off!"

Sasha tore off his arm, and the gun fell to the ground. I loved that dog.

"Get them!" Turner gave orders while he stepped behind his followers.

The group surged forward. I charged into the crowd, brandishing the sword and slicing a path in Turner's direction. Janda had my left flank, and Sasha had the right. Most of the followers fought with their fists, although some had knives. If anyone else had a gun, they didn't use it—not after what Sasha had done.

The drone did a nosedive, spinning as it went. It was another of Turner's bug designs. This one had a mini-drill for a nose that bore into one unsuspecting human who had the bad luck to get between me and the drone. She screeched. The drone backed off and re-routed its trajectory. Now that I knew Turner was using his cell phone to bark directions for the drone to follow, I pushed harder through the throng to reach him. The drone tailed me all the way.

The shifters swarmed in like a badass S.W.A.T. team. I was grateful for the help in clearing a path to reach Turner. The guy was adept at evading capture by shoving one human after another in front of him. The throng of people seemed stunned and floundered in their attempt to fight us. It wasn't much of a fair match, even though the drone swept through our ranks and kept digging into flesh now and then. Turner didn't seem capable of launching more than one drone at a time. That was good news.

Sebastian covered Janda from behind, biting jugulars like it was a feast on Christmas morning. The vamp was enjoying himself. It wasn't often he got permission to devour so much human blood. The laws were pretty strict about such things. He took full advantage of the situation, pausing once to wipe the drips from his lips so the blood wouldn't stain his clothes. He was particular about not soiling his outfits.

The drone made another pass, swooping low and aiming for my chest. It almost hit me before I grabbed it and threw it to the ground. I used the sword tip as a pike that pinned the device to the hard earth, where I stomped on it like the bug it was.

Turner was a few feet away, feverishly pulling another drone from one of his pockets. I didn't give him the chance to set it loose. I smashed into him, knocking him to the ground and sending his phone skipping over the grass near the stone wall. There would be no more drones launched in our direction.

I hadn't been able to use the sword with so many

people around me. I wanted to avoid accidentally cutting into one of our own. But now, I had Stephan Turner where I wanted him. He sat up and scooted backward on his ass to get away from me.

I held the sword over his cowering form. He truly was weak when he didn't have his followers to save him.

"Say hello to your father," I said, gripping the sword and waiting for the vortex to show itself.

My tattoo ached, so that was good, yet it didn't open the vortex. Then I realized the sword had to make contact with the two items acting as keys. Since I was holding the sword and bore the tattoo, the sword would recognize my leviathan cross as being in contact with a source and would allow the first key to start opening the vortex.

Turner, with his coat filled with magical brimstone, was the second key. Sasha bounded over to my side and stood there, growling at Turner.

"Heel," I said. "He's mine. Be a good dog and help Janda."

Sasha gave Turner another growl before racing off to defend Janda.

"You don't want to do this," Turner said. He backed against the wall and tried to creep his way along its border.

"That's where you're wrong."

I brought the sword down and cleaved him in two. There was a resounding pop, and then my world went black.

CHAPTER 34

BACK WHERE I STARTED

For the love of Pete, I was back in the Underworld and inside the demon prince's lair. How the hell had that happened?

Jasper loomed over his son. "You fool. You could have had anything your heart desired."

Turner wasn't exactly alive, but he wasn't dead either. It was odd to see him cut in two and still breathing. The sword hadn't completely sliced him in half. He wasn't bleeding. The blade had effectively cauterized the wound. When he spoke, only half his mouth moved. The other half kind of drooped.

"You're too selfish to give me a single thing. So I claimed what should have been mine." Turner's speech was garbled, but we could still figure out what he was trying to say.

Jasper bent down, grabbed his son by the collar, and dragged him to his dais, where he placed him on a stone table. The demon prince ran his hands along Turner's body with his palms facing down and keeping them just above the body's surface. Heat waves flowed from Jasper's fingers and palms into Turner's skin, which began mending itself. It was freaky to watch.

I backed quietly toward the exit that I knew from experience led to the lava pits. I was hoping the tunnel had been reopened and I could leave.

"Not yet, Smithy," Jasper said.

His back was to me as he worked over his son, but it didn't seem to stop him from knowing exactly what I was doing.

I halted where I was and sighed. "Are you sure he's worth fixing up? He isn't much of a fighter. He's good at running away, though."

"I don't run away," Turner shouted. "I am strategic." His words were no longer garbled, and his voice was stronger.

"Sure, you are," I said. I crossed my arms and leaned against the cave wall, impatient to be on my way home. I still carried the sword, and now that Turner was on the mend, I wasn't so sure I wanted to leave it here. The best idea would be to toss it in a lava pit.

"Smithy," Jasper said. "What did you think of the sword we fashioned?"

"It's balanced, has a fine edge, and is totally unpredictable. However, it didn't perform as expected, or I wouldn't be standing here now. It was supposed to send your son to you and not both of us. You also forgot to mention that Janda's touch would create a vortex."

Jasper, the son of Satan, laughed. "Then it did exactly as it should have done. You were meant to come back here. Janda was just added insurance to make that happen."

"Why?" I pushed off from the wall and walked to the dais. "This wasn't part of our deal."

"No, it wasn't," he said, continuing his mending. "It was a backup plan in case my son didn't survive."

Turner lifted his head to peer at his father. "What the hell? You didn't know if I'd live or die? What kind of bullshit is that?"

Jasper was silent a moment. He finished putting his son's body back together and walked to his throne. He sank into it, exhaustion on his face. His horns dulled slightly. Healing his son had drained him. "I had years to contemplate whether I'd bother with you, Stephan. But I promised your mother, and I always keep my promises."

Turner slid his feet over the edge of the table and hopped down. "You tossed my mother away like a used dishrag. What could you have possibly promised? You never once cared about our well-being." Turner's resentment toward Jasper manifested into smoke that poured from his mouth. It seemed that in the Underworld, Stephan Turner possessed demonic power.

The horns on Jasper's head blazed and not any kind of blaze. This was a white-hot flame shooting upward. The demon prince sprang from his throne and gripped his son by the throat, lifting him two feet off the ground. "You have no right to speak to me so. Your mother was everything to me. I gave her up to save her, you arrogant little shit!"

He tossed his son into the wall. Turner slid to the earthen floor, dazed. Still, Jasper raged on. "Who do you think made sure you had a place to live, had food, had an education and opportunities? You were the one who killed her! I had Alex hunt you down to teach you a lesson. You had to be put in your place and shown you are not yet worthy to call yourself a demon prince. *Now*, you will learn to be a prince!"

This was awkward. I was witnessing a family argument and understood a little more what it was like to be a father to an unruly, unappreciative child. Jasper's methods were harsh, but I couldn't fault his reasoning. Turner had much to learn, and I'd bet anything he would encounter many more of his father's lessons before his time living here was through.

Jasper's flames disappeared. His horns were back to their usual reddish color. He left his son and returned to his throne. This wasn't the best time to approach Jasper with a question, but I had to ask it.

"What happened to the Headless Horseman and Mutther?" I held Jasper's gaze until he waved his hand in a circular motion and one of his viewing windows appeared on the back wall.

The horseman was in the forge room, a chain secured to one leg, working at building a strong fire. Sweat dripped down his back. He had his mask on, which contained the fiery skull.

After seeing what lay beneath the mask, I came to the conclusion that the horseman was a walking corpse that would decay and wither away if he remained in the living realm without his full mask. He had been the demon's assassin and had made the mistake of thinking he could usurp Jasper's authority and rule in the land of the living. He'd have a long time to contemplate where he'd gone wrong.

I turned away from the viewing window and faced Jasper. "What about Mutther?"

"What about him?" Jasper said.

"Where is he?"

"How should I know?" Jasper stepped down the few stone stairs that went from the throne to the ground. He stopped several feet in front of me. His mood had settled to nonchalance now that he'd expended his rage.

His attitude pissed me off. "He sacrificed himself to

bring the horseman through the vortex. Where is he now?" I worked to keep my tone calm and even, but my muscles did the twitching thing when I got too tense.

Jasper sighed and raised his hand to examine his fingernails more closely, as if he were bored by the topic of Mutther. "If he is in the Underworld, no one has come to tell me. Therefore, I presumed he'd passed over the river and went on his merry way to wherever his dragon kind goes."

I knew Jasper was telling the truth. He may omit details or twist the meaning of something, but he always told the truth. The news would devastate Gwenn, but at least she'd know what happened to him.

"Fine. Then there's nothing more for me here. Point me to the way out, and I'll be on my way."

Jasper glanced over his nails at me. "Nothing more? You just got here. Stay and regale me with your adventures with the ghosts. I caught bits of it and found it quite entertaining." He shifted his attention to his son for a moment before returning his focus to me. "I'd like to know more about the magical devices. I found that particularly intriguing."

"Ask your son. He's the one who came up with the idea, which I admit, was rather inventive."

"Hmm. Yes. Quite inventive." He pulled a small beetle from his pocket and placed it on the ground. The tiny eyes glowed yellow, and the legs spread out as it crawled along the dirt floor. Its pincers clacked together as it moved. Then the body twisted until it morphed into a dragonfly and zipped around the room.

"Impressive," I said. "Does that mean what I think it means?"

A slow smile spread across Jasper's face. "Yes."

"Your son stole the technology from you."

Jasper gave a subtle lift of his shoulders, unconcerned that his child had stolen from him, and maybe a touch proud that it happened. "It would appear so. Making these creatures became a hobby of mine. It was Wart who thought to add the brimstone and my magic to bring them to life. These little toys became my companions." He glanced at Turner. "I hadn't thought to teach them to fight. That was Stephan's addition, which I rather like. Cell phones are of no use in the Underworld, but perhaps we can find a new way to give the devices directions."

"Sounds like a father and son sort of thing. Good luck with that." I was more than ready to leave. Let the two figure their relationship out on their own. I had to get back to my family. Janda would be worried I'd gotten trapped here again, and that was not something I wanted. Sure, the sex had been great when she traveled to meet me in the Underworld, but I preferred holding her in my arms in the living realm.

Sasha came speeding through the archway and ran circles around Jasper and then me. I couldn't help but laugh.

Jasper snapped his fingers, and Sasha settled in front of him, staring up into the demon prince's face. "What have you been up to, my little friend? You have been busy sending unnaturals and ghosts back to me." He patted her head. "That's a good girl. Nice job."

Sasha rolled on her back for a belly rub, which Jasper obliged.

"She's a good dog," I said. As soon as I spoke, Sasha got to her feet and pranced over to me. I reached down and scratched behind her pointed ears. She licked my hand and bounded away.

Jasper watched her antics. "She's special—a spirit who

will flit away at a moment's notice to discover fresh adventures. Sasha is owned by no one." He had a wistful tone in his voice, as if he were recalling fond memories.

"I got that impression." I kept an outward calm as I glanced through the archway, a ball of fear forming deep in my gut.

Sasha came bouncing back and hopped from side-to-side. She yipped once and returned to the archway, every bit the guard dog. Her wagging tail gave her away, and I tensed for what was to come.

CHAPTER 35
MINE

Jasper spun around, alerted by Sasha. "Welcome, Janda. Come join us."

My wife strolled into the demon's lair like she'd done it every day. To be fair, she was well acquainted with Jasper and knew her way around the Underworld. That didn't mean I had to like it. I gritted my teeth at her approach and plastered a smile on my face. I couldn't speak. This lovely woman continued to try to send me to an early grave with her decisions and bold confidence.

She spotted Turner and met Jasper's gaze. "Oh. I see he's still here. I thought he was dead. Pity."

Turner got to his feet and started forward. "Shut your mouth, bitch."

I didn't have to go after him. Jasper sent a volley of fire to land directly on Turner's chest, which sent him flying once again into the cavernous wall.

"Manners!" Jasper hissed.

Janda glanced at me, her eyes filled with a silent question. I gave her a quick shake of my head. Her shoulders sagged. Message received. Mutther would not be going home.

She perked up and strode toward me. "I came to see what was taking you so long, dear."

Jasper spoke up. "I'm afraid that's my doing, Janda. We've been catching up. I'm sorry you felt neglected. You're always welcome in my home." He added emphasis to the last bit, brazen in his desire for her.

I wrapped my arm around her shoulder and pulled her close to my side. She had changed into her bike gear, which could only mean she'd ridden Miss Kitty to the opening where Sasha had first appeared. I glanced at the dog. She barked once. Yeah. Sasha showed Janda how to get inside. That meant I could get out. No traveler witch stuff necessary. All we had to do was go on foot. I didn't know how the tunnel they'd come through connected to here, since Jasper had blocked the old one. But if Sasha had gotten her in, then Sasha could get us out. She might even find a new route that Maude could use. I still owed Maude that debt.

"Sasha. Here." Jasper snapped his fingers, and the dog pranced over to him. He reached down and removed the brimstone collar from her neck. "I see you've found a new home. Very well. You have my thanks for staying with me for so long when it's not in your nature."

Sasha jumped up and put her front paws on Jasper's chest. He rubbed her head before making her get off. It was a normal interaction that took me somewhat by surprise. I'd discovered today that demons had hearts and could love just as much as the rest of us. The fact they were pretty screwed up and inherently evil was another issue to deal with on a different day.

Jasper still wanted what was mine. "*Thou shalt not covet*

thy neighbor's wife" was not something demons believed in. Jasper, however, was patient. He'd had plenty of experience with waiting when his father bound him to this lair. I was fairly certain we hadn't heard the last from Jasper. Right now, I wanted my wife out of his house.

"I'd say it's been great seeing you again, Jasper, but that would be lying. Why don't we call it a day so we can go home?" I was honest, which was something the demon valued in himself and in others.

"The sword," he said, pointing to the weapon at my side. "I'll take that now."

I handed it to him. "Just be sure to keep it out of any kids' hands." I gave Turner a meaningful look. "They might get hurt."

Jasper followed my gaze. "I'll keep that in mind."

"I hate to break up this get-together, but my boobs are ready to burst. Time to feed the baby." A small wet spot appeared through Janda's shirt where her nipples grew taut from breasts full of milk.

Jasper stared at her breasts a little too long. "Congratulations on your little one."

"Thanks," Janda said. "She's bound to be an interesting child."

"With you for her mother, I'm sure that is true." He strolled to the archway. "Come. I'll walk you out." He pivoted on his heel and went into the adjoining lava pit field.

I took Janda's hand, and we followed Jasper, ignoring the snide comments from Turner. Sasha pranced ahead of us, chasing embers floating through the air as we passed through the center of the lava space.

Jasper paused near the largest of the pits. If he thought I

was going to jump into one more of those things, he could forget it. This lava was piping hot and not the same as the water lava pit I traveled to enter his forging room. He didn't say a word, just lifted the sword and dropped it into the molten goo. It sank slowly until only the brimstone in the hilt was visible, and then that also disappeared beneath the surface.

"Thanks," I said.

"The weapon was made for you and Janda, not anyone else. I can't have Stephan trying to wield it when its magic is not tied to him. No, Stephan will learn from the ground up how to make his own weapon and impart his magic into it."

Somehow, that didn't make me feel better. The sword was gone. But new weapons? Great. That was not what I wanted to hear. I bit back my comment and followed him to the tunnel we'd used the time Hulda was with us. "I thought you closed this."

He glanced over his shoulder as he strode into the depths of the dark tunnel. "Only a portion of it collapsed. There are different paths one can take to travel in the Underworld. Don't assume that because one way is closed, there are no other options."

He led us to a narrow side tunnel I hadn't noticed when we were here before. He stopped at the opening and kneeled to give Sasha a hug. "You can come visit anytime you wish, my friend. I understand you have chosen a new journey to embark on. Safe travels."

He rose and let Sasha go. She raced into the tunnel and back again then barked at us.

"That's our cue," Janda said, stepping forward into the darkness.

My tattoo blazed with pain. I grabbed my chest and stared at Jasper. "What's going on?"

"The sword is gone. You no longer require a key. I can't allow you to continue to bear the leviathan cross."

The pain was blinding. I struggled to remain standing and had to place a hand on the warm rock wall of the tunnel. I gulped deep breaths until the pain faded. Janda appeared at the entryway.

"What's wrong?" She rushed back to me.

I breathed in through my nose and out through my mouth. My eyes watered from the force of the tattoo being ripped from my skin. "Nothing much. Jasper decided now was a good time to remove the tattoo. It's all good. I'm good. Nothing to worry about."

"For crying out loud, Alex. It's a tattoo. How bad can it be?" She pulled the fabric of my shirt away from my chest and gasped. "Okay. I take that back. Your skin is beet red." She spun to face Jasper. "Did you have to make it this painful, or is this your idea of fun?" Her temper flared, causing her glow to emerge.

Jasper put up a hand. "Stop. It's not a simple matter of removing a tattoo. This one contained some of my magic, which also had to be removed. It can be uncomfortable, but it's necessary."

"Can be? That's an understatement." I couldn't believe he was so callous about it. Then again, he was a demon.

Janda glared at him.

"You asked for a weapon. I gave you that weapon," Jasper said. "Nothing is free. If pain is the price you pay for your loved ones, is that asking too much?"

I straightened and pushed the pain to the back of my mind. "No. It's not. Thank you."

The demon prince inclined his head and stepped back from the tunnel. "Stay on the path or face what lurks in the shadows. That's my warning. Farewell, Janda and Alex. Take care of Sasha."

We entered the tunnel, walking carefully through narrow sections that had us squished together so as not to veer from the path. At one point, I had to move Janda behind me and we had to go single file until the way widened again.

I wondered if Jasper had set us on an endless trail to nowhere. "Is this the way you came in?"

"I think so," Janda said. "It's hard to tell, but Sasha knows where she's going. Just stick with her."

"Where is she?" This was bad. I'd lost sight of Sasha. "Wait. I don't see her. Let's stand here a moment and listen for her."

We stopped our progress but kept on the path. Eerie moans resounded in the distance. I glanced at Janda. "Right. Keep moving."

"Sasha. Here, girl. Where are you?" Janda called to the dog. "Dammit, we haven't even gotten out of the Underworld, and we already lost the dog. Jasper won't forgive us if anything happens to Sasha."

"She's a free spirit, remember? Just keep going. She'll show up."

I held Janda's hand and led her farther down the tunnel. Now and then we caught glimpses of shadowed movement on either side of us. Instinct told me this would not be a good place to be if we didn't find our way home. We pushed onward, still not seeing Sasha through the dim light. I glanced behind us. That way was worse with all the creepy stuff waiting beyond the trail. There was no way to tell for sure how far we'd come, but going back to get Jasper's help was not an option.

Woof!

Sasha padded toward us, nudging our legs.

"I think she's trying to tell us which direction to go." I was grateful the dog had returned and was more than willing to let her guide us out of this dreary place. She nudged us some more, pushing us to the right. I glanced down at my feet to be sure we hadn't left the path. "It's good. Keep going." I pulled Janda alongside me once the path widened enough for the two of us to continue side-by-side.

"This is right," Janda said. "I recognize this part. It's getting brighter."

She jogged ahead, keeping pace with Sasha. I was proud that I only panicked once when Janda slipped from view. She rounded a corner, and even though she was a mere foot in front of me, I lost sight of her. It was some type of optical illusion that would easily mess with your sense of direction if you weren't aware of what was happening. It was like being in a carnival fun house with mirrors strategically placed to mess with you.

"Over here," Janda said. She stood looking upward. "This is how we came in, but how do we get out?"

We were back at the location where I'd fallen down the pit the first time I'd come with Sasha. "I know this place. Come on. It's this way."

Unfortunately, this tunnel would not be an option for Maude. The narrow pathway, and what waited beyond it, would be too dangerous for her to use. At some point, I'd have to get word to her about it, and let her be the judge of its dangers.

I guided Janda through the narrow space that Sasha

had shown me before and found the ledge stairway that would lead us to the top of the pit. Like earlier, I bounded from ledge to ledge, crisscrossing my way upward. Behind me, Janda imitated my movements. Sasha was way ahead of us, but it didn't matter. We were home.

We emerged to a chorus of celebratory whoops. The bright light blinded us until our eyes adjusted. Everyone was there. Damon hurried over and grabbed Janda in a bear hug.

"Thank God, you made it. I was beginning to think we'd have to come down there after you, but Silas said to have patience." Damon released his niece so Gwenn could give Janda the baby.

Gwenn glanced at the opening behind us. "He's not coming, is he?"

"I'm sorry," I said.

She sniffled, wiping away tears. "I'm not surprised, but I had hoped to see him."

"Yeah. I know. Me, too." I gave her a hug. "I wish things were different. You'll always have us, Gwenn. Always."

She smiled just a little. "Thanks." She joined Janda and Wrenley, who were surrounded by the rest of our extended family.

Damon came over to me and shook my hand. "Thanks for bringing my girl back home."

"I think it was more like her bringing me home. You should have seen her striding into the demon's lair to get me. I didn't mention it to her, but she had some of the witch's glow coming off her. She was magnificent. Even Jasper couldn't keep his eyes off her until she calmed down and the glow dissipated."

"Yeah," Damon said, gazing at his niece, "she's pretty

special. Never saw anything quite like her until now." He was smiling at Janda and Wrenley.

I followed his gaze and realized he was right. Wrenley was just like her mother. So much so, it made my heart ache with happiness. This was my family—shifters, vampire, witches, and now a magical dog.

Boom! Boom!

Everyone sprinted away from the blasts that came from behind me. I whirled around to see rocks flying in the air and crashing down into the crevice we'd emerged from moments earlier. Fire seared through each nook and cranny. The blaze grew so intense I had to step farther away from it. Orange, red, white. The flames melted the stone. I didn't know a stone could do that, but it did.

We gathered together a safe distance away to witness the sealing of the portal to the Underworld. It seemed the demon prince wanted no more unexpected visitors in his realm. Or else he wanted to be sure to keep certain hostile elements, like the Headless Horseman or Stephan Turner, from getting out. Either way, I was fine with this pathway being closed forever.

As I gathered my wife and child into my arms, a thought struck me. Jasper said that even though one path may be impassable, there were always other ones to follow in the Underworld.

The hairs on my arms stood up. I hoped no such paths would be found for a very long time so my daughter could grow up unbothered by the things that went bump in the night.

The dust settled, and the temperature fell to within normal range. It was time to go. One by one our friends and family said goodbye. Damon, Silas, and Nick gave permission for everyone to leave. Some shifted to run through the woods of Sleepy Hollow while others wandered back to their cars and trucks to drive away. Sebastian kissed the heads of Janda, baby Wrenley, and Gwenn—the ones he cared about the most in the world—marking them as his own.

He left slowly this time, walking deeper into the woods, most likely to spend some time at the ruins of Hulda's hut. He'd sit on the stone wall there and tell his beloved all about the newest witch in her family and how he wished she was still here to see the baby. Someday he would leave this world and join his true love in the spirit realm, but not until he was done protecting Hulda's heirs.

Shawn had brought Angie with him in his police cruiser and offered Gwenn and Sid a ride home. I watched them leave and felt the tug of grief that Mutther wasn't with us anymore.

The day was especially warm for this time of year. The sun beamed down on my faithful friends as they waded through tall grass and wildflowers to reach the trail that would take them to where everyone had parked.

I took a moment to stand in awe at my surroundings and was grateful to be blessed with the privilege of enjoying it for yet another day thanks to the sacrifices of my family and friends.

Despite the losses we'd suffered, nature lived on, bringing new life into our world for us to enjoy and cherish. My daughter, conceived in the Underworld, was proof that something good could come from even the most unimaginably dismal of places. She had the same glow as her mother and would certainly share that with others who sought a way through the darkness to find peace and comfort in the afterlife.

Part of me was scared for them both. Their gifts were a

mixed blessing. Yet, another part of me was proud of who and what they were—a guiding light of love.

I put aside my worries for another time. Today, I wanted nothing more than to be with my new baby and Janda. I kissed my beautiful wife—the woman who captured my heart the first day I met her in a paranormal hotel that knew better than the two of us that we belonged together.

AUTHOR NOTES ABOUT THE BOOK

Alex's story had to be told. So much happened to him in the Underworld that shaped his life—like conceiving a child.

Sleepy Hollow and its paranormal inhabitants are seen through his eyes. I wanted to share this perspective with readers. His hopes and fears about becoming a father are very real for every father.

Alex witnessed the demon family dynamics and was surprised by the love, dysfunctional as it was, between the demon and his son. Much like real life, good can be found in the shades of gray to remind us that not everything is as it seems. We're complex creatures.

I explored the theme of family so Alex's character would demonstrate growth in love and friendship.

The historical facts in this story were more about the area in Sleepy Hollow. The water tank does exist just as described.

The ending was to pay tribute to all the characters from each of the Sleepy Hollow Hunter books.

I hope you've enjoyed this series and found the characters to be endearing enough to stay with you long after the final page was read.

Thank you for spending time in the world of Sleepy Hollow Hunters.

Also by Sheri Queen

Discover the other books in the Sleepy Hollow Hunter series and other stories by Sheri Queen. Please note, the heat level rises as the Sleepy Hollow Hunter series continues and the characters commit to deeper relationships.

SLEEPY HOLLOW HUNTER SERIES:

Bounty Huntress (Sleepy Hollow Hunter Book One)

Brimstone (Sleepy Hollow Hunter Book Two)

Pirate Lover's Curse (Sleepy Hollow Hunter Book Three)

THE NIGHT ACADEMY SERIES:

Wolf's Bane (The Night Academy 1)

https://books2read.com/sheriqueen

If you enjoyed this book and want to know about exclusive deals, upcoming reveals, and extra content, join the Sheri Queen community newsletter.

https://sheriqueen.com/pages/subscribe

You'll automatically receive stories when you join!

ABOUT THE AUTHOR

Sheri Queen writes immersive stories of adventure and romance.

Her contemporary fantasy and paranormal women's fiction stories feature snarky bad-ass women, strong female friendships, found family, and steamy romance.

Sheri received her MFA in Writing Popular Fiction from Seton Hill University. She grew up in the Hudson Valley region of New York—an area she loves to depict as a back-drop for her stories—and enjoys traveling to new places where she is constantly discovering inspirations for her writing. She especially loves visiting old graveyards.

https://sheriqueen.com/

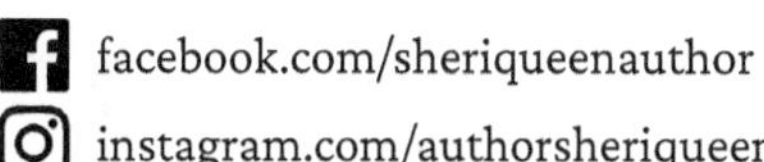

facebook.com/sheriqueenauthor
instagram.com/authorsheriqueen